He Knows the Way

A Christian Romance Set in the Tumult of 1960s Mississippi

By Idella Borntrager Otto

TriedGold Publishing LLC

Copyright © 2017 by Idella Borntrager Otto

TriedGold Publishing LLC

ISBN **978-1-9758649-7-2**

Contact author at idellaotto43@aol.com

book and e-book designed and formatted by
ebooklistingservices.com

1 3 5 7 9 10 8 6 4 2
Printed in the United States of America

Dedication

To Emory, the love of my life
who has faithfully
traveled the Way
with me

Acknowledgements

I would like to thank all the gracious people who made it possible for me to research, write and edit this book:

Emory, my best friend and writing coach, for his patience, editing suggestions and technical support. I couldn't have done it without you.

Maria, our daughter, who helped keep the household running smoothly during hectic writing days.

Thanks to my delightful editor, **Jeanne Leach** whose expertise helped navigate me through the perils of historic Christian fiction and the nuances of the English language. It was a joy to work with you.

Stella Kauffman's original song "Lord, as I Walk with Thee." Reprinted from *Life Songs No.2*. Copyright 1938 Mennonite Publishing House. Adapted by David R. and Ruth Miller , 1965. Used with permission from Menno Media/Herald Press.

Thanks to my research cohorts **Amy Wallace Pauls, Marie Wallace, Larry and Maxine Miller, Dennis and Viola Miller, Floyd and Lois Borntrager,** and **Glen and Emma Myers**. Your input was invaluable.

I am very grateful to **Amy Deardon** from EBook Listing Services for walking me through the publishing maze.

Cover photo image courtesy of Gitchell's Studio/Eastern Mennonite University. Shenandoah yearbook 1968.

He Knows the Way

CHAPTER ONE

Mississippi, Summer of 1965

M iles out on Choctaw Ridge, a share-cropper boss man's pickup truck came barreling toward Ellen Yoder in the opposite lane, carrying three white men with farmer's hats pulled down over their faces. The hats obscured their identities. The obvious display of guns was unnerving. Despite the ninety-eight-degree weather, she shivered.

"They must be going out to hunt wild pigs."

She turned left at the gravel Forest Road intersection where lush green Kudzu vines lined deep roadside ditches on either side.

The first shack was Will and Shonia Tatum's. Pulling into the rutted driveway, she parked her sporty silver VW Beetle.

Gathering her purse and her "English as a Second Language" teaching materials, Ellen glanced into her rear-view mirror. The men in the battered red pickup had turned around, followed her, and were now parked crosswise in the road. Her skin went clammy and the muscles in her neck tightened. Three hundred feet away, the truck blocked her return route to Missula.

The three of them, in their tee shirts and dirty jeans, cigarettes dangling from the corners of their mouths, stood beside the truck and stared at her. Each held a shotgun, barrel to the ground, but it would only take a second for them to aim the guns at her. Their anger and resentment reached across the distance like a bolt of electricity as they glared at her through their hatred. Once more she glanced into the rear-view mirror. Ellen was certain she saw one of the men brandish his gun at her. Were they merely trying to intimidate her, or did they plan to do away with her like the Ku Klux Klan eliminated the three Civil Rights Workers last summer? Goose bumps snaked up her arms.

Determined to keep her teaching appointment, she opened the VW's door and slid out. Keeping her eyes averted, she forced herself to move toward Shonia's front door. *Oh Lord, protect me. Protect Shonia and her family.*

With each step, the dry red clay dusted Ellen's sandal-clad feet. A black turkey buzzard with its sharp, hooked bill, made a silent nosedive for its prey lying in green grasses under a towering pine tree at the edge of the un-kept yard. Still, she walked on. Her back prickled with an awareness of the men's hostility. Did Shonia and her Choctaw Indian family live with this threat hanging over them every day?

The stately pines whispered in the late afternoon breeze. Was this really happening out on Choctaw Ridge with its blue, picture-perfect skies?

Crossing the threshold of the sagging porch, she knocked on the screen door. Nothing. Usually Shonia was right there, welcoming her with a smile in her luminous dark eyes. Ellen knocked again. And again. Still no answer.

Was she not home or did those men with their guns intimidate her too much to acknowledge the white woman on her porch? Shonia was never late getting in from chopping cotton in order to be on time for her next English lesson.

Bewildered by Shonia's absence, Ellen retreated to her car. No way could she get around the pickup to return to Missula. Neither was it safe for a white woman to take the road in the opposite direction which led into the remote Choctaw forest. Besides, Ellen had forgotten to fill her car with gas. The gage indicated it had already switched to the small ancillary gas tank as she drove onto Choctaw Ridge. She could get to Missula via the usual route but wouldn't make it through the thirty-mile stretch of no man's land.

Sitting in her car, Ellen prayed as she had never prayed before. *Heavenly Father, these men in front of the pickup are frightening. They have guns and have their sights on me. I need your protection, right now, Lord!*

She lost track of time as she prayed. She was in grave danger with no means of communicating for help. Lifting her head, she glanced over her right shoulder and was shocked and relieved to see the pickup had vanished. The vehicle was a dusty red color, like a dozen other farmers' trucks traveling these rural gravel roads. She wished she had recorded the license plate number.

Since Shonia had no phone, Ellen considered leaving a note. She quickly abandoned that idea lest she jeopardize her student's safety. Should she report the harassment of the armed men? If so, to whom? She had a feeling the Missula police wouldn't cotton to the idea that she was teaching English to the Choctaw chief's daughter-in-law. After all, local wealthy cotton farmers depended on the dirt-cheap labor of the share-croppers, whether black or Indian. Was that what upset those men?

Ellen wasted no time leaving the Ridge community. As she drove, she struggled with how to handle what had happened. Was it a random thing that those men followed her, a young Mennonite missionary, into the Choctaw community? Did they resent her teaching because they saw her as a symptom of the forces trying to undermine the economic fabric of their lives? What would Nesimba and Noxumpa counties be like if most of the marginalized population became literate?

Or had she been specifically targeted for some reason? Had the men followed her knowing who she was and where she was going? Ellen reached the parking lot of the Missula Nurses' Residence and looked over her shoulder, but didn't see any trailing vehicles. She peered around every bush and tree as she hurried inside to the haven of her bedroom.

Ellen checked her watch. She had two hours before needing to prepare for work as the night nursing supervisor of Missula General Hospital. Maybe a nap would ease the tension that had followed her home. She lay down and tried to relax but kept feeling the men's animosity and seeing the guns in her mind.

After ten minutes, she gave up. If only she could talk to Rachel Mishler, but her meager salary wouldn't stretch to pay for an optional long-distance phone call to Indiana. Ellen remembered her best friend's reaction when she told her where she was being assigned by their denomination's mission board.

"Not Mississippi!" Rachel cried. "It's so violent there. You know what happened just last summer."

Perhaps Ellen should've listened to her. She sat up and grabbed a piece of stationery.

Dear Rachel,
You won't believe what happened today...

After she'd written about her visit to Choctaw Ridge, she felt better. Oh, the men still concerned her, mainly because they were representative of the way too many Mississippians thought, but they didn't seem as menacing here in the safety of her bedroom.

What she'd written would likely scare Rachel who worried too much about Ellen. *If I send this, she'll get all protective and urge me to leave what she sees as a dangerous place.* She scrunched the letter into a ball, then pitched it into the waste basket.

When she went to the closet to get her uniform, the beautiful Choctaw dress Shonia had made for her caught her eye. She ran her hand over the lovely hand-stitched appliqués and colorful beadwork. Smiling, she pulled on her uniform. Tempers might simmer too close to the surface at times, but God had called her here, and she wouldn't be scared away.

CHAPTER TWO

W ork. Sleep. Work. Like a gerbil on its exercise wheel, Ellen felt caught in the endless cycle of duty. By eleven p. m., she was back at work, listening to a thirty-minute report from the previous shift and then made rounds.

Now that work at the hospital required so much of her energy, she questioned her bi-vocational call to serve on a part-time basis at Missula Mennonite Mission. She wrestled in prayer while checking on patients.

God, I feel drained from the constant demands of being a Yankee supervisor in Confederate territory. Not only was she new at this nursing supervisor's job, but she perpetually stepped on someone's Southern toes. *Lord, give me the wisdom to get through this night without alienating anyone.* Her experience today out on Choctaw Ridge and the lack of sleep added to her weariness.

She recalled the night they ran out of linens on the "black" hall. Ellen had gone to the linen closet on the "white" hall to get sheets to change a black patient's soiled bed. She had become the target of an angry verbal barrage.

"You can't take that linen for niggers!" demanded the LPN who worked as the medication nurse.

"Pardon me, ms., I need to use this bedding. Like you, I am concerned that we have enough linen for everyone until eight o'clock in the morning. But there's no way I'm going to leave a patient in distress simply because of the color of his or her skin.

"Right now, our nurses' aide is busy in the nursery, so I'll change this bed for her. Excuse me, please. I have a task to do and I believe you have medications to pass out."

Lord, you created each person. Why should I be criticized for taking linen from the "white" closet? It all seems so arrogant and absurd.

That happened several nights ago, but the incident still bothers me.

Midnight approached. Ellen followed hospital protocol and checked the white patients first. Then she turned her attention to the black hall. As she finished rounds, the ER buzzer shattered the quiet in the nurses' station. Startled, she jumped up and rushed back to the Emergency Room entrance where she expected to see a patient requiring immediate medical attention.

Instead, Barry Chupp and Dixon Weldy were opening the trunk of Barry's car at the ER entrance. Like Ellen, the two young Mennonite men were part of the Missula Mission Team in addition to working at Missula General.

"What are you guys doing here?" she asked. "Aren't you scheduled to be on duty in the morning?'

Barry waved to her. "Come here. You may want to check this out."

Without hesitation Ellen stepped next to the open trunk. She gasped!

Stark terror swept over her as she glimpsed the charred remains of a burned cross lying in the dark cavern of Barry's trunk. She often felt like a novice when trying to interpret the Southern mindset, but this was the first sign of impending Ku Klux Klan violence.

Barry's forehead was furrowed and his jaw set.

"Where did you find this, and why are you bringing it here?" she asked. The darkness edging the hospital perimeter could be holding a thousand unseen eyes. In the floodlights of the hospital entrance, she could be the next target.

Barry spoke in hushed tones. "Were you out at Shonia's today?"

"Yes." Ellen's stomach tightened, her mouth dry as a cotton ball.

"I went out for her weekly English lesson, but for the first time ever, she wasn't there." What does that have to do with this?' Her question was abrupt.

"Maybe nothing. But on our way back from our English sessions on Choctaw Ridge, we saw this smoldering cross at the intersection leading to Will and Shonia's. Did you see anything unusual while you were out there today?"

Ellen felt the blood drain from her face. "Yes, as I turned onto Choctaw Ridge, a red pickup truck raced toward me. It held three men with guns." She paused. Her hands shook as she rubbed her forehead. "I passed them thinking they must be out hunting wild boars."

The night air held a thick, suffocating humidity. Her knees were weak. She thought she might collapse. Leaning against the car, she steadied herself.

"As I got out of the car, I could see this same pickup parked crosswise in the road, which blocked my return to Missula. It was strange and scary. When Shonia didn't answer her door, I went back to the VW and began crying out to God for protection.

"By the time I lifted my head, they were gone. I drove back to Missula without incident. So, you think that's the reason for this charred cross?"

"It may not have anything to do with it, but given the location and timing of the burning, we had better not discount it." The lines in Barry's forehead softened. "I wouldn't go out on the Ridge alone, if I were you."

Dixon, the philosophical one, stepped out of the shadows of Barry's vehicle. "I have a hunch that you've just been tagged as another Civil Rights Worker like the five hundred plus college students who invaded Mississippi last summer. Since they managed to mobilize the black community for voter registration and education, white landowners are not eager to watch their Choctaw workers follow suit."

"But I'm not a Civil Rights Worker per se. All I'm doing is teaching Shonia to read."

Dixon shrugged. "To the white landowner, it's one and the same."

Barry closed the car trunk with a thud. "We don't want to detain you, but we felt we should warn you."

"Thanks, guys, for warning me. I've got to get back to work." Shaken, Ellen retreated to the ER entrance and was relieved to hear the doors locking behind her.

Ellen's shift passed in a blur. She had difficulty concentrating on the patient charts on her desk. The smell of the ashen remains and the visual image of the cross plagued her. Would she become just another statistic like the murdered white Civil Rights Workers Mickey Schwerner and Andrew Goodman and their black friend, James Chaney—all casualties of last summer's infamous "Mississippi Freedom Summer?"

A scripture text from the book of Job nibbled at Ellen's mind like a broken record. *He knows the way that I take and when He has tested me I will come forth as gold.*

Lord, did I misread your leading to serve you in Mississippi? I don't need to be gold. Silver or pewter would be just fine.

Ellen lowered her head and covered her face with the palms of her hands. She could be married to John, safe back home. But they didn't share the same life goals of missionary service, so she'd walked away. She sighed deeply. Going solo was a lonely road. She'd never imagined that answering God's call to serve in the deep South would be so difficult.

The absence of John's calls and their dates, created a void. Ellen missed belonging to someone who, in turn, belonged to her. Being half of a couple had fulfilled her need to be cherished.

Sometimes being single was good, like making her own choices in her own time. Yet, she couldn't deny that she wished she had someone to share her fears, someone to share her heart.

Throughout the wee hours of a very long night, the events of the past twenty-four hours replayed nonstop in Ellen's mind. Her shoulders slumped and her usual perky walk slowed to one degree above a shuffle. At her desk, she propped her cheek with her fist. *Maybe, just maybe, doing what I can to relieve the abuse of others is worth the risk.*

CHAPTER THREE

*E*llen needed to let go of the night's frustration and deal with the probable danger of returning to Choctaw Ridge. *Brother Don—he will know what to do. He's been the pastor of Missula Mennonite Mission for two decades.* Like most Mennonite pastors, Don Mast preferred to be called "Brother Don", since the denomination views the church as a brotherhood of believers versus the designation of a clergy hierarchy.

Dialing Brother Don's office, Ellen hoped he would be in. She was relieved to hear his familiar, "Hello, Don speaking."

"Would you have time to talk if I stopped by this morning?" Fear of being overheard kept her from explaining her dilemma. What if the KKK had tapped her phone line?

"Yes, I plan to be in the office all morning." Brother Don didn't press her for details.

"See you in twenty minutes." Ellen changed out of her uniform in a scant two minutes. She slipped into a casual blue floral skirt and crisp white blouse, and removed her nurse's cap. Sleep would wait. She gulped down a glass of milk and a cinnamon roll. Not very nutritious, but she could run on adrenalin. Grabbing her keys and purse, she headed out the door.

Brother Don ushered her into his modest home-office. A bookcase along the opposite wall held volumes of commentaries, Bible translations, and well-worn study materials. An ample oak desk, scarred by years of use, sat in front of the books. The adjacent wall with a large picture of Jesus holding an injured lamb, lent an atmosphere of peace and protection to the room. Ellen needed that peace.

"Come in, come in. What brings you here when you probably need to be sleeping?"

Ellen collapsed onto a nearby, well-worn couch. She wanted to close her eyes, but her mind was racing. Her words were propelled by her pent-up emotions. "Yesterday I was out on the Ridge for Shonia Tatum's English lesson. You know Shonia. She's different from many of her peers. She's always there and always on time when I come."

Brother Don leaned forward in his antique desk chair. "And. . . ?"

"And en-route to her house, I was met by this red pick-up with three gun-toting men." Step by step, she recounted her previous day's experiences, including the appearance of the charred cross which Barry and Dixon found near Will and Shonia's house.

"What's going on, Brother Don? I'm not a Civil Rights Worker. I'm simply teaching my friend Shonia to read so she can read the Bible for herself and possibly help her family rise above their level of poverty."

Brother Don tilted back in his creaking chair, tapping his fingers on the desktop. "Barry and Dixon are probably right. You're a young Yankee professional who recently came into the area. You are being targeted because the landowners see you as a Civil Rights Worker. You've also befriended Chief Tatum's daughter-in-law, not an insignificant person by-the-way. People must have found out you are teaching her to read English.

When Mississippi was inundated last summer by northern 'do-good' college students, most of those students arrived with Yankee tags on their vehicles." Brother Don paused, "Ellen, do you still happen to have a northern license plate on your car?"

She bolted upright. "Yes. I haven't bothered to apply for a Mississippi tag since state law grants me five more months to make the switch. So, you think that's part of the problem? From the landowner's perspective, I guess I do fit the Civil Rights Worker profile." Ellen clasped her hands together so tight, the knuckles were white. "So, now what do I do to protect both Shonia and me?"

Brother Don's furrowed forehead and penetrating gaze heightened her anxiety. She did a fast mental calculation. It had been a mere fifteen months since the murders of the three Civil Rights Workers.

Brother Don hesitated.

She waited.

"Ellen, I know you have a passion to teach Shonia to read. But be very, very careful. You are part of our mission personnel, so I would request you not go out on the Ridge alone or after dark. We don't know when or where the KKK will strike. You'll need to apply for a Mississippi license plate as soon as possible. I don't want to see you get hurt."

Ellen nodded, absorbing her pastor's instructions and his concern. She was aware that the fear of an economic upheaval drove some landowners to join the mushrooming KKK, perpetrators of the violence. Thus far, newspapers had reported that in the civil rights murder trials, only eight of the twenty-five Klan suspects had been brought to justice.

"Thanks for your advice," she said. "I'll follow your instructions."

She hesitated. Perhaps she'd better tell him everything. "Several nights ago, I was checking the babies in the nursery. The black nurse's aide, who cares for the infants, had overheard the white LPN giving me a hard time for using linen from the "white" side to change the bed of a black patient. We had run out of linen on the "black" side.

"In low tones the aide said, 'Ms. Yoda, y'all be real careful. I ain't tryin' to make no trouble, but when black folk axe too many questions, dey burn our churches. Ma'am, you stan up fo us blacks an y'all's church might burn too.'" Ellen stared at the pastor. "Do you think she's right?"

Brother Don's smile showed his sadness. "The aide's warning is partially correct. To date, seventy Mississippi churches—most were black—have gone up in smoke. Some of the churches were bombed or burned to intimidate. Some have been destroyed out of vengeance. Since we, Mennonites, have taken a stand for non-violence and have refused to become involved with the KKK, it is conceivable that we too, could become a target.

While we need to be careful not to antagonize those who differ with us, fear of reprisals can't be the basis for our decisions. You did the right thing by meeting the needs of a patient, without respect to color."

"Thanks, Brother Don. I've heard you preach that all men are created equal by God. So, it wouldn't be right for me to discriminate between white, Choctaw, or black. I've also heard you say, the way of love is stronger than the way of hate and violence. It's living it that's hard for me."

Her pastor nodded. "I'm not into marches or politics to force change in Mississippi. But I do agree with Martin Luther King, Jr. when he says, 'Darkness cannot drive out darkness, only light can do that. Hate cannot drive out hate, only love can do that.' Sorry, Ellen, I didn't intend to give you another sermon."

She managed a wry smile. "Right now, I needed that reminder in order to stay sane in this insane world."

Ellen rose to leave and shook her pastor's hand. "Thank you so much for taking the time to answer all my naive questions. You have been very kind."

Mid-morning heat blasted her face as she exited the air-conditioned office and walked to her car. *Will I need to take the heat of even more discrimination against Shonia and her people? What if I put both of us in harm's way by going back out on Choctaw Ridge? But I must find a way, or Shonia will think I've abandoned her.*

As the attractive, young nurse drove away, Brother Don stood at the window. He had the distinct impression Ellen could be someone his son, Lamar, might be interested in dating. *Where did that thought come from?* He shook his head like a confused spaniel. Brother Don had no intention of becoming a matchmaker for any of his children, especially not Lamar who was not due to return home for another year. But in his last letter, Lamar had written, "Dad, it's lonely out here." Don was right proud of his son who was involved in a three-year service stint in the Belgium Congo under PAX, the Mennonite equivalent of the Peace Corp.

Lord, keep her safe. Ellen has a gentle heart that connects with the Choctaws and her patients at the hospital. She's beginning to understand our racial tensions which can erupt without warning. And Lord, if it's your will, could you reserve her for Lamar? In Jesus name, Amen.

CHAPTER FOUR

O n the way back to the nurses' residence, Ellen reflected on what brought her to Missula. Four years prior, her extended family had moved from a racially integrated community in Michigan to Mississippi to assist in the development of two churches. She had opted to remain up North to follow her life-long dream of becoming a registered nurse.

Now, a nostalgic smile graced her lips as Ellen drove toward Missula. She recalled earlier times of attending Missula Mennonite Mission during her nursing school vacations. Ellen had chosen to accompany her older brother's family to the rural Choctaw mission church while her parents attended a sister congregation in town. She and Shonia Tatum, the Chief's daughter-in-law, were drawn together by some invisible bond that defied southern cultural boundaries.

Shonia had a patrician air about her yet was never arrogant. Her straight, black hair glistened like pure onyx in the sun. She always reached for the pew Bible, even though her reading ability faltered, having only the equivalent of a second-grade education.

Seeing her friend struggle to find Brother Don's sermon text, Ellen whispered, "Shonia, Matthew five is on page seven-hundred-twenty."

Shonia flashed an appreciative grin. Her passion to learn English permeated every aspect of her life. At the close of the service, she asked, "You show me how to use Bible?"

"Shonia, I'm not an English teacher, but I'll try." Shonia's desire to know more of God and her engaging personality drew Ellen to her.

After dismissal, while other women organized a potluck fellowship meal, the two friends escaped to a quiet Sunday school classroom.

Ellen began with the basics of demonstrating the difference between the Old and New Testaments. Sixty-six books in the table of contents posed the first big challenge. Shonia spotted the Old Testament book of Jonah and the New Testament gospel of John.

"Two Johns?" she giggled.

"No, old Jonah and new John," said Ellen. They laughed.

Time together was cut short by a call to lunch. Entering the noisy lunch line, Shonia sang quietly, "Old Joe and new John."

Before leaving for home she checked with Ellen. "Tomorrow, I chop cotton till three o'clock. Then you come? Show me more Bible?"

"I'll come," replied Ellen.

Later, she wondered whatever possessed her to say yes? She's not a linguist.

Even though Ellen had misgivings, she was at Shonia's by three p.m. the next afternoon. She remembered climbing the uneven steps to the front porch. How sad that her friend's family needed to live in a tenant shack that hadn't seen even a hint of repairs in eons. Shonia and her husband, Will, worked hard to eek-out an above-poverty living, but never succeeded.

In response to her first gentle knock, Ellen could hear quick footsteps on the interior bare floor. The door swung open to reveal Shonia's dark, eager eyes and welcoming smile. "Come in."

Her gentle beauty had a way of dispelling her bleak surroundings. She led her guest to an old table with two unmatched chairs.

Not knowing where else to begin, Ellen asked, "Shonia, is there a certain part of the Bible you want to get to know?"

"Yes. God so loved—where to find?" Shonia picked up a tattered Bible, the only visible reading material in sight.

"We can find that Scripture. Let's go back to the table of contents with the page numbers. Remember the book of John?"

A smile of recognition broke on Shonia's face. "New John."

"You're right. New John, chapter 3 and verse 16. Let's read it together."

In halting English, Shonia followed her mentor's diction, "For God so loved the world, that he gave his only begotten son, that whosoever believeth in him should not perish, but have everlasting life."

Tears glistened in Shonia's eyes. "God so loved Shonia . . . he gives me life."

Ellen hugged her friend. During subsequent school breaks to visit family, Ellen visited Shonia to assist her in mastering other parts of her treasured text. Their friendship flourished like southern azaleas, in spite of long absences when Ellen needed to return back North to nursing school.

On the heels of her nursing school graduation came the phone call which would forever alter her life.

"Ellen, this is Matthew Troyer from Rosedale Mennonite Missions."

Ellen sucked in her breathe. She'd completed the lengthy application process for a foreign medical mission assignment, and it had been approved. Brother Troyer must be calling to clarify whether she was being assigned to Costa Rica or Belize, her first and second choices for missionary service. Ellen could visualize the astute, balding, mission executive who'd interviewed her with kindness and perception.

"I know you were counting on a Central American assignment," he said. "But we have an urgent need for a registered nurse at Missula General Hospital in Missula, Mississippi. If you opt for this assignment, you would also become part of the mission team at Missula Mennonite which has a Choctaw audience. I believe you are familiar with the setting."

Her heart stood still. What was Brother Troyer asking her to consider? "Yes, I'm quite familiar." Ellen tried to keep disappointment out of her voice.

"We have several other nurses who are willing to go to Central America. But none of them are as familiar with the southern culture as you are. Since your family lives there, you are the most qualified person for the Mississippi position."

She scarcely registered the rest of the conversation.

"I'll be back in touch within a week," he said in an upbeat tone. "Missula General has requested that a Mission-appointed RN report for orientation as the night supervisor in two weeks." Brother Troyer took a deep breath. "Sometimes, Ellen, mission begins at home."

Ellen let the receiver drop back into its cradle. Yes, she was quite familiar with the setting. On her last Christmas visit, she decided it was fine for her family if they wanted to bury themselves in the Deep South. But rinky-dink Missula? No way. Mississippi, with all its racial and ethnic discrimination was not where she wanted to invest her future. The tee shirt that read, *this isn't the end of the world but you can see it from here,* described her exact sentiment.

She placed a frantic call to her best friend. "Rachel, I've just received a call from Matthew Troyer asking me to go to Missula, Mississippi, instead of Central America. What do I do now? Except for my passport and six weeks of orientation at Mission Headquarters, I thought Central America was a given."

Tears of utter dismay coursed down Ellen's face. "I really don't want to get caught in the middle of all that black-white-Choctaw chaos." Her voice held a tremor. "Dad says James Meredith has already stirred up a lot of animosity with his civil rights march from Memphis to Jackson. I just want to serve somewhere in a quiet spot of the world where I don't need to worry about all the hassles of integration. There's going to be more trouble in Missula. I just know it!" Ellen poured her frustration into Rachel's listening ears, thankful for such a caring friend.

When Ellen finally took a breath, Rachel said, "Ellen, right now it feels like your world has turned up-side-down. Let's meet at my house tonight at seven. I'll call Ann and Loralie. We'll talk about the possibilities and pray with you."

That night, the tight circle of four friends spent time talking, fasting, and praying for direction for Ellen.

Then half-way through the week, Ann asked, "Have you considered that God may be redirecting you to Mississippi at this particular time?"

"I've thought about it all right. And I don't want to go there."

Back in her apartment Ellen tried to sleep but tossed and turned. A strange thing had occurred. She remembered how Shonia Tatum's face kept appearing in her mind again and again as she and her friends prayed for direction. The question she had relegated to the far corner of her mind could no longer be ignored. What if God wants me in Mississippi, and I'm being a Jonah, running from the racial tension I fear? Hours later, she slipped to her knees, ready to do whatever God asked of her. The Holy Spirit had nudged her in the direction of Missula. Bit by bit she opened her clenched fists, releasing the more enticing dream of a foreign assignment. She had tried to ignore the Scripture text, "He knows the way that I take. . ." but it confirmed for her that God wanted her to embrace the need in Mississippi.

Now, given the threat of the three men in the red pickup and the charred cross, Ellen wondered if she had made the right decision.

CHAPTER FIVE

A week passed after the cross-burning incident. Her Mississippi license plate would not be available for another seven days.

Ellen called her parents' home. Mrs. Yoder answered.

"Hello Mom. Would it be okay for me to borrow one of your cars to go see Shonia since my license plate hasn't arrived yet?"

"You certainly may use one of our vehicles, but are you sure it's safe for you to return to the Ridge?"

"No, I'm not certain, but I think I need to return for Shonia's sake. Mom, would you consider going with me?" Ellen was confident she could rely on the support of her parents whose life purpose included bringing the gospel to Choctaws.

"Well, I would rather go with you than sit here and wonder if you're safe."

"Thanks, Mom. I'll be at your house in thirty minutes."

They left town, chatting about Mother-daughter topics as though they had no great concern.

Twenty miles from Missula, Ellen turned onto the Ridge. Their chatter ceased. Both watched every vehicle and scanned the passing landscape. "Mom, let me know if you see anything unusual."

"I've not seen anything like the red pickup or other signs of possible violence. I think we're safe with our Mississippi tags."

At the Tatums,' Ellen retraced her steps across the ramshackle porch to Shonia's front door. Her mother waited in the car. The porch roof sloped on the south end where a post had given way.

Ellen's knock brought no response. A painful lump formed in her throat. There was no sign of life inside the curtainless window. She could envision the two-room interior, lit by a single light bulb suspended from the ceiling and its walls papered with old newspapers like many share-cropper shacks.

Where was Shonia? Ellen checked her watch. Usually she was in from the fields by this time. Just to be sure, Ellen skirted the back of the house. Perhaps she was doing laundry in her barren back yard.

She called, "Shonia. Shonia." Only silence reverberated in the late afternoon heat.

Maybe her friend was so busy working, she'd lost track of time. Scanning the endless cotton fields that bordered the property, Ellen couldn't detect Shonia's distinctive profile. The young woman had a characteristic rhythm of hoe down and hoe up, weeding the continuous rows of green, that would form white cotton bolls, and create white gold for the white land owner. Will and Shonia were to be given a "share of the crop" for their labor. Shonia rarely complained, but that portion was never enough to help them rise above poverty. They were bound to a pitiful existence on the land that once belonged to the Choctaw Nation.

Ellen trudged back to the car, shoulders drooping. Tears threatened to spill down her cheeks as she opened the car door and slid behind the wheel.

"Why, Mom? Why? When Shonia was doing so well? She was excited about learning to read English. In church, she was beginning to comprehend which passage of Scripture was being read. I can't believe she's choosing to end her lessons."

"We don't know all the reasons as to why Shonia isn't here," her mother said in a calm, rational manner. "I'm sure she was aware of the cross burning which was meant to intimidate both you and the Tatums. The KKK knows we won't be asking too many questions. You can be sure that whatever threat prompted Shonia's absence, the price tag was too high for her to have been here."

With reluctance, Ellen headed the car back toward home, certain another Choctaw dream had just been thwarted by white man's greed and lust for power.

Mother and daughter fell silent.

Ellen thought of a recent speech by black civil rights activist, Dr. Martin Luther King, JR. when he said, *we must accept finite disappointment, but we must never lose infinite hope.* While she hadn't lost hope in an infinite God, Ellen wondered what hope there'd be for Shonia's future.

Today was so different from her previous visits to Shonia's house. Each time she knocked, the door creaked open to reveal Shonia's radiant black eyes. Dressed in native Choctaw garb, she invited Ellen into her home with a smile and a hearty "Welcome, friend." Ellen always felt welcome in this modest home. Once, Ellen had admired the intricate hand-work of Shonia's red and white Indian outfit, complete with a white ruffle-edged apron. "Shonia, how do you make the ruffled edging surrounding the yoke of your dress and circling the bottom of the full-length skirt? You have dozens of little white hand-stitched triangles forming a border next to the edging."

Shonia's face lit with an effervescent smile. "You like? Come. I show you."

She led Ellen to a scratched, antique treadle sewing machine, reminiscent of something Ellen had once seen in her grandmother's basement. Shonia carried herself with a certain grace and tall dignity ascribed to her as the wife of the chief's son.

"You teach me English. I make you Choctaw dress," Shonia declared.

Ellen had wanted to protest, but something told her this was a sacred moment. Was she, a white Yankee Mennonite nurse, being accepted as one of them? Ellen flicked away unbidden tears. Choctaws were a reserved Native American Nation and did not lightly admit others to their inner circle.

Not wanting to be a financial burden to Shonia and her family, Ellen hesitated. "Shonia, if I buy the fabric, are you saying you will make a Choctaw dress for me?"

"Yes. You buy. I make." Excitement danced in her eyes.

A week after the purchase of the soft blue cotton fabric for the dress and white for the decorative apron, the outfit was finished, complete with a multi-layered beaded necklace.

When presented with the gift, Ellen was speechless for a moment. It took her breath away. What had she done to deserve this kind of sacrificial love-gift from Shonia? She had wanted to laugh and cry and dance at the same time. She touched the exquisite appliqués on the dress and fingered the hand crafted necklace, which spoke volumes of unusual acceptance. Tears threatened as she reached out and hugged her friend. "Thank—thank you, Shonia," she murmured. "You must have worked long into the night to have completed it so quickly. It's beautiful. I'll be right proud to wear it to the Choctaw Festival."

Shonia beamed. This hallowed moment cemented their friendship.

Today, while driving back to Missula, Dr. King's powerful, *I Have a Dream* speech echoed in Ellen's mind. In his booming voice, he declared, "I have a dream that my four little children will one day live in a nation where they will not be judged by the color of their skin but by the content of their character."

It didn't seem to concern many people that Shonia and her people were persons of dignity and First Nation Americans. Their brown-toned skin glistened daily with the sweat of white oppression. Sometimes being a peace-loving Mennonite, left Ellen with more questions than answers.

CHAPTER SIX

C oming home from the fruitless drive to Choctaw Ridge, Ellen stopped to check her mail. She recognized the characteristic flowery script of her friend, Rachel, on one of the envelopes. Scanning the letter's contents, her spirits lifted.

Dear Ellen,

You promised to be my maid of honor before leaving for Mississippi. I can't imagine going through this momentous life transition without your stabilizing presence to keep me on track.

Dear Rach and her superlatives.

> *I'll ship the fabric and pattern. I'm sure your seamstress mother will do a superb job of fashioning a just-right dress for you. You'll be stunning in the gorgeous, pink, silken creation.*
> *Do say you'll come.*

The letter contained a few more details, which she read quickly.

"Yes, Rachel. I'll come," Ellen mused out-loud, glancing around the entryway of the Nurses' Residence to see if anyone was listening. She could feel the tension of the past two hours seep away from her taunt shoulder muscles.

Almost dancing down the hallway, she gently tapped three short raps on Anne Maria Schrock's door. The two nurses worked opposite shifts, so they devised a quiet knock which would not disturb the other in the event one was trying to catch an extra hour of sleep before reporting for duty.

Her Missula Mission co-worker's door swung open. "Come in, Ellen. What brings you here?"

"A delightful letter. Remember, I mentioned my best friend, Rachel, who is engaged to her childhood sweetheart, Dale Stutzman?"

Anne nodded.

"Well, she's reminding me I promised to be her maid of honor when they get married in two months. There's just one problem. I'm sure I'll need coverage for several night shifts at the hospital. Would you consider being my back-up if the Director of Nurses can't find enough nurses to fill in while I'm gone for a long weekend?"

"I'll be happy to be your back-up. Don't waste time fretting about coverage." Anne Maria's heart was as generous as a Mississippi spring rain.

"Thanks so much. I'll fill in for you when you leave to visit your family in Ohio. I can't wait to see Rach and the rest of the gang. The next two months will seem like forever and a day."

Anne Maria laughed. "You'll live, my friend."

"Yeah, I'll live, but I'll be counting the days until I leave.

On the runway of the Delta airliner bound for Fort Wayne, Indiana, Ellen turned to wave goodbye to her parents. This was her first flight, heightening both her excitement and apprehension. She was relieved when the seat beside her remained empty. This would give her undisturbed "think time." Perhaps no one would notice her uncertainties.

Turning to the window, Ellen scarcely noticed the stewardess in the trim blue-green Delta uniform serving the perfunctory soda and pretzels. They were flying above an enormous bank of cotton ball clouds that had just been milled by the Creator's gigantic cotton gin. *Hmm, this is so unlike earth-bound cotton fibers. There's not a speck of dirt or leaf or burr appearing in God's cloud formations.*

Above the clouds rose the vast expanse of clear blue sky. *God, you must have arranged this breath-taking scene to remind me of your limitless love for me.* She would need that reminder within the next twenty-four hours. *What will it be like to be in the same social circles that John and I moved as a couple?*

Today she was flying to northern Indiana. Rachel was marrying Dale, the man of her dreams which made it almost perfect. It truly was an honor to be a part of Rachel and Dale's inner circle, but Ellen's bittersweet thoughts lingered. How would she feel walking down the aisle as the maid of honor when it could have been her wedding day? But John's world and hers were going in two different directions. Their life goals didn't mesh. Mission, particularly medical mission, was not on his horizon.

Would she always be the maid of honor? *God, I long to love and to be loved by the person you've chosen for me.* She'd heard John was dating someone else now. I wish them well, but I miss not having someone with whom I can share my future.

Ellen arrived at Rachel's home the day of the rehearsal and fell right into the whirlwind of wedding preparations.

"Ellen, you're here!" Rachel squealed and ran over to Ellen. They hugged as if it had been years since they'd seen each other.

"Let me show you my dress, and we can pick up the flowers to decorate the reception hall, and check on the cake, and meet Dale and Duane for lunch, and be at the rehearsal by 4 p. m. and—"

"Whoa. You're going to run out of 'ands' or oxygen pretty soon." Rachel's exuberance was infectious. Ellen loved every minute of it.

The rehearsal proceeded without a hitch. Ellen's escort, Duane Miller, was a comfortable friend she had once dated casually. Coming from the same youth group, he was aware of Ellen's past relationship with John and put her at ease.

Ellen felt secure and feminine in the dress she was to wear in the wedding. Rachel had forwarded the beautiful silken fabric to Mississippi, which Ellen's mother fashioned into a perfect fit for the maid of honor. The sweetheart neckline maintained her modesty while the pink fabric and tulle sash skimmed her slim waistline. Her street-length, gathered skirt swirled softly over a nylon net petticoat.

Ellen would have preferred to wear a floor-length gown. However, Conservative Mennonites considered formal dresses extravagant and following worldly fashion trends. Rachel chose to adhere to church guidelines. Perhaps the denomination would soften that tradition in the future. Ellen hoped so, because she had her heart set on wearing a long white bridal gown if, or when, her special day ever arrived.

Dressed in pastel blue pajamas, Ellen sprawled across the bed. She cupped her chin in her hands, observing Rachel prepare for bed. Her friend was floating on Cloud Nine.

"Rachel, your smile reaches from ear to ear. What's it like to be almost married?" Ellen basked in her friend's happiness.

"Oh Ellen, it's anticipation of what will be and a hint of fear that I won't be able to live up to Dale's expectations of a Godly wife. I feel over-the-top happiness and a smidgen of regret that I'm trading in my single freedoms for married togetherness. Being almost married is knowing beyond any doubt that I love Dale and that he loves me.

"I can't believe this is the night before our wedding. At this time tomorrow, I'll be Mrs. Dale Stutzman. We'll never again need to say goodbye. We'll be together always. Did you want me to extol the virtues of marriage for the next four hours?"

"Spare me, please." The friends giggled.

Rachel sobered. "Ellen, I need to tell you something. John and Marian will be at the wedding. They've just announced their engagement."

For a split second, Ellen's breathing suspended. She put her fingers over her mouth and bit her lower lip as if to trap a painful comment. "I had a feeling it might happen and I wish them well. But seeing them together will be a jolt. Thanks for filling me in before tomorrow." She sighed. "Rach, do you think I'll ever find the right guy and get married?"

"Of course, you will. You're already two-thirds married."

"What do you mean by that?"

"You're willing, and God's willing. All you need is for some guy to wake up and become willing."

Eventually their alternating laughter and serious moments ceased. The two drifted off to sleep.

An *a cappella* ensemble in the balcony sang "Tread Softly" in melodic harmony as Ellen made her way with sedate steps to the front of the sanctuary.

Standing next to the groom at the altar, six-foot, wavy-haired Duane smiled his encouragement. His expression told her, *Ellen, you can do this.*

Turning to acknowledge the bride's entrance, Ellen's eyes met John's briefly before he averted his gaze. I wonder what he's thinking? Does he have any regrets? I don't. Ellen had prepared herself for the possibility of this moment. Her intact smile never left her face.

Rachel's radiant appearance in her white satin wedding dress, obliterated the uncomfortable moment. The ceremony was both sacred and joyous. Sacred, as they exchanged their memorized vows. Joyous, as the bride and groom blended their trained voices, singing a magnificent harmonious duet to each other;

"LORD, AS WE WALK WITH THEE FROM DAY TO DAY
TEACH US TO LEARN TO LOVE THY BLESSED WAY.
WHEN WE WOULD WANDER, LEAD OUR ERRING FEET.
HOLD THOU OUR HANDS 'TILL JOURNEYS ARE
COMPLETE.

WHEN IN OUR PATH THE CROSSROAD LIES AHEAD,
HELP US TO CHOOSE THE PATH THAT WE SHOULD
TREAD;
SO, MAY WE WALK THROUGH GLADNESS AND
THROUGH TEARS,
GUIDE THOU OUR FEET THROUGHOUT THE PASSING
YEARS.

AS IN THE EVENING WHEN WE TRULY SAY,
WE IN THE PATHS OF GOD HAVE WALKED TODAY.
SO, MAY WE SAY IN THAT LAST DAY TO GOD,
LORD, IN THY WAY WE HAVE FOREVER TROD."

Walking out of the sanctuary on the arm of the handsome best man gave Ellen an opportunity to regain her inner composure.

Duane spotted John and Marian in the receiving line. He nudged Ellen and gestured discreetly so she'd look that way. He leaned down and whispered, "You'll do okay."

She smiled her thanks and turned to greet Marian and John. "Congratulations on your engagement. And best wishes on your future together." Her sincere greeting came from deep within and surprised her.

John's anxious expression relaxed. Perhaps his uneasiness had exceeded Ellen's apprehension. Seeing the two together was not as difficult as she thought it would be. *Lord, I haven't a clue as to what lies ahead for me, but I'm ready for my marching orders.*

CHAPTER SEVEN

Between the excitement of the wedding and the flight back to Missula, Ellen was exhausted. But she had little time to recoup before she needed to report for duty. Since her absence had created a staffing shortage at Missula General, she worked non-stop for the first week and a half after returning home.

On her first night off, Ellen forced herself to stay awake until eight p.m. to ensure a night of uninterrupted sleep. She finally crumpled into bed. Ah, what bliss! I can sleep for the next twelve hours.

The phone jarred her into semi-wakefulness. Had she just fallen asleep? Ellen attempted a bleary-eyed peek at her bedside clock and groaned. The round Little Ben registered a green luminous one-thirty a. m. Who would be calling her at this unearthly hour other than Missula General's ER?

She reached for her bedside phone. "Hello," she croaked.

"Ms Yoder," the night nurse's urgent voice jolted her awake. "I'm so sorry to call you, but we need someone in the ER stat to assist Dr. Percy with a trauma patient. There's been a two-car crash. I can't leave the floor because we have a patient in hard labor. I've checked the nurses' on-call list and we have no one else who will cover. Can you come?"

Now fully awake, Ellen jabbed the switch on her bedside lamp which cast a low-beamed glow on the light green walls of her sparsely furnished room in the nurses' residence. These days, everything "hospital" was painted light green. Her bedroom hadn't escaped the pervasive anemic green paint brush.

Her feet hit the floor. "I'll be there in five minutes."

She slipped into her ever-ready spotless white uniform and gave her long, luxurious dark-brown locks a swift "updo." She secured her white nurse's cap with the narrow black velvet band firmly to her head with bobby pins. The front of Ellen's uniform displayed her name tag and her nursing school's gold pin, indicative of her professional status as a registered nurse.

Grabbing her black woolen nurse's cape, Ellen's emotions ran the gamut from mild to strong annoyance. "Don't I deserve a night off?" she muttered to herself. "I've already worked nine consecutive nights."

But the neophyte supervisor's sense of responsibility propelled her into action. She sprinted across the lawn from the nurses' residence to the hospital emergency room entrance. Ellen shivered in the black night due to the adrenalin racing through her and the damp Mississippi wind whipping under her cape.

Garrett, the orderly posted at the locked metal doors, watched for her through the glass windows. He opened the door before she could reach up to ring the ER buzzer. Even in the midst of a trauma scene, he acknowledged her rank. "Ev'nin, Ms. Yoder. So sorry to awaken you. Good of you to come. Ma'am, we shor do need your hep."

Ellen smiled and nodded at Garrett's obvious relief. In the past, he had declared, "Ms.Yoder, when you're in charge of this hospital, it runs smooth as melted butta." He was a responsible young man who liked order, not chaos.

Striding into the brightly lit emergency room crowded with accident victims on this frigid winter night, Ellen assessed the scene unfolding before her. With the evaluating eye of an "in charge" nurse, she dashed to the end gurney in the curtained divisions of the white-tiled emergency department.

Tall, gaunt Dr. Percy hovered over a Caucasian woman writhing in pain. The patient was hemorrhaging from her injuries. Ellen was relieved to see Dr. Percy on duty. He was the newest, most gentle doctor in town, and she surmised also the most competent to handle this situation. Her fatigue and annoyance evaporated as Ellen moved swiftly into her familiar nurse's role, including a fast hand scrub.

The ER admission chart at the head of the stretcher identified the patient as Mrs. Charlotte Grason. While checking the patient's wavering vital signs, Ellen glanced at the doctor. "How can I help you most, Dr. Percy?" she asked quietly.

The physician straightened and smiled his thanks. Glancing at the nearby IV pole supporting a liter of fluid, he said, "Her patent veins are almost non-existent, but it's running. Dixon will be here soon from the lab with the results of the type and cross-match for the first unit of blood. We'll need to get it going as quickly as possible."

Ellen didn't dare leave the bedside even for a second as doctor and nurse worked frantically to stop the patient's bleeders. Few words were exchanged while they worked in sync. She was poised to take one instrument from the physician's hand and with her other hand, slipped the next instrument into his fingers. The unbroken rhythm of two minds and four hands was like the dance of fluid choreography as they raced against the clock to stop the bleeding and ease the pain.

Within minutes, Dixon appeared from the lab with the unit of blood.

"Thanks, Dixon. I'll hang it at once," Ellen said. "It appears we'll need more units. Do we have more available?"

"Yes. I'll type and cross-match several in advance. Just buzz me when you need them."

Ellen hung the life-giving fluid, but the hemorrhaging was relentless. She called Dixon for more blood. As one unit emptied, she added another.

Beads of perspiration appeared on Dr. Percy's forehead. Ellen wasn't certain if it was due to the precarious condition of the patient or the chain-smoking physician's need for another cigarette.

If onlys raced through Ellen's mind. If only the patient was stable enough to be moved to Meridian's Trauma Center. If only an IV pump was available to speed up the flow of the current transfusion.

Dr. Percy, who was accustomed to improvising, looked up. "Ms. Ellen, put a pediatric blood pressure cuff on the unit of blood and pump it in by hand."

For the next five or six hours, whenever the blood flow slowed, Ellen carefully increased the pressure in the cuff.

Doctor and nurse worked like a scripted professional pair, stitching up the external wounds while monitoring internal injuries. The ashen face of the now unconscious Mrs. Grason, was a mute reflection of her blood pressure that kept plummeting into the double-digit danger zone.

"Pardon me, ma'am." Ina, the housekeeper entered the curtained enclosure.

Ellen stepped aside only for a moment to make room for Ina, who gathered the used instrument packs encased in green surgical linen, bound for the autoclave.

Ina's job description held no boundaries. As a black domestic, she was at the mercy of her white supervisors. Ellen wondered what thoughts and emotions the ever-placid housekeeper had. Besides her duties in the ER, she cared for the newborns in the nursery and served as the night shift cook. The dependable employee could deliver collard greens and scrumptious fried chicken in short order. Ina never questioned the requests of her white supervisors, but Ellen wished she could somehow alleviate the hollow pain she often witnessed in Ina's eyes.

Ina's multiple skills and compassion reminded Ellen of her northern friend, Joetta. Joetta and Ellen connected in geometry class when the Michigan high school integrated. During lunch breaks, the two friends tutored basketball players, lest they be kicked off the team for low math scores. Joetta went on to graduate valedictorian. No one stopped to ask whether her skin was white or black. If only Ina could be given the same consideration. She had the skills. Why should nine-hundred geographical miles make such a difference when the same laws regarding a person's rights were on the books?

Six hours passed since the race to save Mrs. Grason's life began. Rays of dawn filtered through the venetian blind slats of the ER windows. The patient began to stabilize. Her vital signs inched up into the near-normal range when her eyes blinked open in total confusion.

Ellen stepped up near the patient's pallid face, and said in a gentle, reassuring voice, "Mrs. Grason, you've been in a serious auto accident, and you are in Missula General Hospital. You're going to make it. Your husband and daughter were also injured, but they will be alright. For now, you can rest."

With that, the patient relaxed, closed her eyes, and drifted back into the sleep of pain-medication-induced oblivion.

After he stitched up the last of the jagged cuts on Mrs. Grason's mangled lower left leg, Dr. Percy stretched from his cramped position. He cocked his head and grinned. "Ms. Yoder, if I were a doctor and you were a nurse, we'd make a team!"

The day shift arrived, ready to assume the care of the patient.

Ellen stepped out of the ER entrance into the cold, misty morning almost euphoric in knowing she had been part of a life-saving team. Yet as she headed home to an empty apartment, the sense of great accomplishment left a void within her. Something inside her longed for a special someone with whom to share this moment. *Lord, it's time I put such thoughts behind me and concentrate on being content with where you have me right now.*

CHAPTER EIGHT

Sunday Morning

Driving into the church yard, Ellen pulled up next to the aging, faded blue, Missula Mission van and parked. It was splattered from the hubcaps to the roof with red Mississippi mud. Barry had returned from making his usual Sunday morning run to pick up Choctaws living beyond walking distance. He slid open the van door as Ellen stepped from her VW.

"Good morning, Ellen," Barry called.

"Good morning, Barry."

Will and Shonia Tatum, along with ten-year-old Missy and eight-year-old Willete exited the van. With only the toes of their shoes showing below billowing red skirts, Willette and Missy giggled with abandon as they dashed to meet their cousins clustered at the church entrance. A smile flitted across Shonia's face as she watched her daughters. They were two little tulips bobbing in an early springtime breeze.

Ellen walked over to Shonia, relieved to see her again and wanting to give her a big welcome hug. Instantly Shonia's expression became guarded. She stood erect and unmoving.

Ellen kept her feelings of concern in check. "Good morning, Shonia. I've missed you so much. Are you okay?"

Shonia looked to Will. Not a word was spoken, but Ellen detected a definite note of caution passing between them.

Shonia stared into space. "I had to work." Her words came out just a bit above a whisper.

"Shonia, you're reading so well. I'll be glad to come next week, or we can arrange a different time." She dared not ask the avalanche of questions flooding her mind, lest they be overheard.

Shonia's eyes glistened with unshed tears as she shook her head ever so slightly with finality. "No, I'll need to work."

"I understand, Shonia." But she didn't understand. "I'll still be your friend."

"Thank you." With that Shonia turned and with resolute steps, walked toward the chapel.

Ellen heaved a deep painful sigh. She had just lost something very precious. Not only was she losing the privilege of being Shonia's tutor, but she was also being shut out of a dear friendship.

Not wanting to make Shonia uncomfortable during the worship hour, Ellen sat across the aisle and a bench behind the Tatums. This morning they were in full Choctaw garb, complete with multi-colored beaded necklaces. Will sported an identical form of Shonia's intricately woven beadwork, except his necklace was two inches wider, which Ellen recognized as the masculine version. His crimson shirt with matching white diamond trim on the yoke, identified him as a "right proud" Choctaw. Missy and Willette wore miniature carbon copies of their mother's outfit. What an impressive family!

After the morning service, Ellen approached her former student. "Shonia, on Tuesday afternoon I'll be going to Louisville to pick up Sunday School materials for church. Would you like to ride along to do some shopping for your family?"

Shonia made no reply. In the past, she'd been eager to accompany Ellen on any shopping excursion. She looked at the floor, then turned her back and began an animated Choctaw conversation with her sister-in-law.

Ellen was nonplussed. Something or someone had erected an intangible wall of fear around Shonia. She suspected it had something to do with the burning cross. Or was Shonia being harassed by her white boss man again? Was she being intimidated to relinquish the dream of becoming a literate Choctaw? Perhaps, she would once again be subjected to becoming the boss-man's "convenient" mistress. Shonia had already mothered one "mulatto" child. Everyone could see that Willette's lighter skin and shining long, black hair branded her as a mix of Choctaw and white lineage.

Was it guilt that drove Shonia to favor Willette over Missy? Will simply tolerated the child, much like he had tolerated the boss man's sexual harassment, convinced they had no choice lest their meager income be totally cut off. After the Tatums became believers, Brother Don became aware of their plight and confronted the landowner. Will had assured Brother Don the sexual seduction had ceased. Now Ellen sensed that a recurrence of such harassment had become a real possibility.

Ellen checked her side-view mirror as she turned the VW back toward town. The mirror reflected the small chapel whose only external décor was a four-foot wooden cross above its front entrance. Here was where Ellen found a shelter for her troubled thoughts. Here was where Choctaw and white could sit side by side as one unified brotherhood without fear of someone saying, "Move! You don't belong here."

This morning every available spot in the sanctuary had been filled with eighty worshippers singing hymns in Choctaw and English. Teens and children spilled into two attached Sunday school rooms. Native American and Caucasian frequently found a safe haven within the chapel walls. But today, Ellen left with an unsettled feeling of being on edge. Something wasn't right.

CHAPTER NINE

Weeks passed. Ellen missed the tutoring sessions with Shonia. She experienced an even keener sense of emptiness that was precipitated by Shonia's distant friendship. Mid-summer air simmered and cooked with heat.

One evening Ellen received a phone call from Brother Neal Ginder, who served as senior pastor of Missula's sister Choctaw Mennonite Church at Pine Ridge.

"Ellen, my family needs a break before we begin two intense weeks of Vacation Bible School. We would like to visit family in Maryland next week. I know you are very busy but would you consider helping us next Sunday? It will mean teaching the six to eight year olds and leading singing during the worship service.

Our daughter and their two small children will accompany us to Maryland. Dean will stay at our house, preach the morning sermon and drive the church bus run." Brother Neal paused to give Ellen time to consider his request. Dean was Brother Neal's son-in-law and served as the bi-vocational associate pastor at Pine Ridge.

Ellen wavered. She needed to work Saturday night from eleven p. m. to seven-thirty a.m. Sunday morning. Her greatest fear was falling asleep at the wheel while driving thirty miles from Missula to Pine Ridge for the ten o'clock service. "I would be happy to assist with teaching and the music. But would you mind if I brought my six-year-old nephew, Anthony, with me if his parents agree? He could help me stay awake." To go for a jaunt with Aunt Ellen was a treat for Anthony who perpetually begged for a ride in her little silver VW that had a novel sun-roof. Besides, Anthony would get to be with his little buddies at Pine Ridge.

"Oh, that would be fine." Brother Neal sounded relieved. "Mr. and Mrs. Jim Meuller will also come to assist with teaching Sunday school.

Now I have another huge favor to ask of you. Dean's vehicle needs major repairs. He typically uses it to drive to his summer school teaching position at Riverdale High School. Since we will need our car to make the trip to Maryland, would your car be available as a "loaner" during our absence? The Meullers have offered to provide transportation for you back to Missula."

Ellen never hesitated. "Certainly, I will be happy to leave my car for Dean's use." Due to the abrupt cancellation of Shonia's English lessons, Ellen had no great need for a car during the coming week. She could walk across the lawn to work and had only two blocks to the nearest grocery store. It was not unusual for the staff of the sister churches to work together to meet whatever needs arose, be they personal or mission related.

By Sunday morning the humidity lifted. Clear blue skies and bird songs seemed as buoyant as Anthony's, "Hey, Aunt Ellen," as he slid into the bucket seat beside her.

"Hey, Anthony." Ellen never failed to enjoy Anthony's bouncy, little-boy exuberance.

His mother called her instructions from the front door. "Remember, Anthony. Don't distract your aunt too much while she is driving. Have a good day!" She waved, and then disappeared into their ranch style home. With that, they were off to Pine Ridge.

Anthony's observant chatter ranged from, "Aunt Ellen, look at the pretty fawn beside the road," to "I think I hear the sound of a dove."

Ellen slowed for a stop sign. She had no trouble staying awake with her nephew's running commentary of the passing landscape. Then Anthony stopped in mid-sentence. He cocked his head to look at the side view mirror. He frowned.

"Aunt Ellen, why is that car with six men following us?"

"I don't know Anthony, but I noticed they've been following us ever since we entered the Nesimba County line. Maybe they just happen to be going the same way we're going." Ellen doubted the validity of her own statement but she didn't want to alarm Anthony. The tail-gaiting vehicle remained within a car length of her back bumper for miles.

Nearing the church, Ellen caught a glimpse of the gleaming white chapel situated on the Ridge in an isolated clearing amidst the Choctaw pine forest. A quarter mile before the church, they passed Brother Neal's modest frame home. In front of the house there were deep ditches, over-grown with kudzu vines creeping up both sides of the tree lined gravel road. An access drive had been excavated across the ditches to create an entrance to the Ginder's tidy, picturesque home. A warm welcome emanated from the pastor and Mrs. Ginder whenever one stepped inside the unassuming four-room bungalow.

As she rounded the bend, Ellen breathed a sigh of relief once the church's arched entry-way came into full view. Each Sunday morning, Brother Neal or Brother Dean would be on hand to greet the worshippers as they entered the archway before passing through the white double-doors into the pine paneled sanctuary. This morning there was no one to greet them. The car followed her to the church parking lot entrance; slowed, then cruised on by. Ellen mentally tried to dismiss it as mere coincidence.

Anthony jumped out of the car the minute it came to a complete stop. "Where's the bus, Aunt Ellen?" Next to little silver VWs, Anthony loved big busses—school busses, church busses, Grey Hound busses—any kind of bus fascinated him. Besides, his Choctaw buddies would be on the church bus.

"I don't know where Brother Dean is with the bus. Perhaps he needed to wait on someone to get ready. You know Choctaw time is a bit different from white folk time. I'm sure he will be here within the next thirty minutes or so. Let's go in and say 'Hey' to all the folks that are here."

The elderly Jim and Janice Meuller sat in the midst of twenty Choctaws that had walked to church. Greetings of "Hey, Ellen" and "Hey, Anthony" echoed throughout the sunbathed sanctuary. When the bus arrived there would be another round of forty more warm greetings. Ellen and her shadow, Anthony, made their way to a front bench. A superb blue and red beaded Choctaw cross highlighted the front of the polished pine pulpit. This morning it quieted Ellen's swirling thoughts in the tenuous Mississippi atmosphere.

Thirty minutes passed with no sign of Brother Dean and the bus. Someone suggested they sing. Ellen led the group in singing for another thirty minutes. Without warning, the sanctuary doors burst open and a bus load of Choctaws streamed into the building. Brother Dean was the last to enter.

He strode toward the pulpit and Ellen quickly took her seat. There was a respectful silence as Brother Dean stepped behind the podium. Ellen had never seen the unassuming Brother Dean so shaken. Even his knees seemed to tremble. His hands gripped both sides of the pulpit. His eyes thinly veiled the gravity of his next words.

"You've wondered why I was late in picking you up this morning. I promised to explain once we arrived back here at the Chapel. Early this morning I got up to review today's sermon. I stepped into the bathroom and a shot rang out. The bedroom window was shattered as a bullet from a high powered rifle whizzed into the headboard of the bed. It grazed the pillow where I had been laying just minutes before.

In light of recent Civil Rights incidences in our county, I notified the Sheriff's Department. They came to do an initial investigation. I was informed they could do very little to help since the only evidence they have is the bullet casings. I'm not certain who would be targeting me. I do know that people in the school system have been very disturbed because I refused to discriminate against black and Choctaw students in my classroom. I may lose my teaching position for the coming school year." His voice broke.

Brother Dean guided the congregation in a time of urgent prayer for safety for each of them in the coming weeks. Even small children sat quietly and snuggled close to a parent or older sibling.

After dismissal, there was a low buzz of concern among the adults. Children scattered outside to play until they would be called to re-board the bus.

In hushed tones, Ellen approached the Meullers and Brother Dean. "This morning I was trailed by a car-load of men starting at the Nesimba County line to the church parking lot. Maybe it was happenstance, but it made me feel uneasy."

"Jim, I would suggest you follow right behind Ellen over to Dad and Mother Ginder's where she plans to leave her car for my use this week," Brother Dean said. "Anthony could ride from the church to the house with the Meuller's so Ellen's transfer to your car could be accomplished more quickly in case our movements are being watched. The danger may have passed but we can't be sure. Let's not take any more chances than necessary."

Brother Dean left to transport the Choctaws to their homes while the Meullers and Ellen secured windows and locked the church.

CHAPTER TEN

*A*nthony hopped into the back seat of the Meuller car. Ellen and the Meullers eased their vehicles onto Pine Ridge Road in tandem. Ellen's heart lurched. Facing them beside the road, the tail-gating vehicle was parked on the far side of tall shrubs bordering the parking lot. It took a scant five minutes for her to pass the car and reach the Ginder driveway. She stopped, locked her car, and ran to the Meuller sedan bound for Missula.

By then the pursuing car had made a U-turn, forcing Mr. Meuller toward a deep embankment. Not knowing if there would be gunfire, Jim commanded, "Everyone, get down!"

Mrs. Meuller crouched beneath the dash. Ellen pulled Anthony down with her between the seats, cradling him in her arms. Shock, fear and confusion registered in Anthony's dark eyes. Ellen held a finger to her lips as Anthony edged even closer into her protective embrace.

Jim managed to keep his car from rolling into the ravine, righting it back onto the roadway. The pursuing vehicle dropped back two car lengths, following the racing Meuller sedan to the county line.

"They've stopped following us. I think we are safe," Mr. Meuller cautiously exhaled.

"Thank you, Jesus," exclaimed Mrs. Meuller. Ellen echoed the older woman's praise as she and Anthony wiggled up onto the back seat.

Anthony began to cry. "Anthony, it's Okay. We're safe now." Ellen tried to reassure her nephew as he clung to her. Gradually she could feel the tension in his little-boy-body relax when there was no further sign of the pursuing vehicle.

"What were they going to do to us," queried Anthony.

Ellen shrugged and said, "I don't know Anthony." She was bewildered as to what the motive of the men might be.

Mr. Meuller came to her rescue. "Son, I'm sure those men are up to no good. Brother Dean told me last week that he accidentally found a moonshine still in the woods near Brother Neal's house. He called the police because it is against the law to make what we call moonshine or whiskey. The police came and destroyed the still. Since we are Brother Neal's friends, I think those bootleggers were trying to threaten or scare us away."

"Aunt Ellen, what's a bootlegger?"

"Anthony, a bootlegger is someone who makes or sells whiskey without a license, which is against the law. Do you remember when your buddy, Tommy, stayed at your house for a while when his daddy got drunk and beat him and his mother?"

Comprehension crept into Anthony's eyes. "Oh, so bootleggers sold Tommy's daddy some moonshine and he got real mean."

"Right! Then our family and the whole church began praying that Tommy's daddy would become a Christian and stop trying to use moonshine to forget his troubles. Your Daddy and Bother Don became close friends with Tommy's father. They told him the good news that Jesus could help him fight the urge to drink moonshine. What is Tommy's daddy like now?"

Anthony grinned at his aunt. "He's not mean any more. Sometimes I and my Daddy, and Tommy and his daddy go fishin'." Anthony settled back into his seat, content to know that his world was secure, at least for the moment.

The Meullers and their passengers arrived home without further incident. Ellen arranged to call her sister-in-law while Anthony was doing chores in the barn with his daddy. Ellen didn't want to increase the trauma for her nephew but knew she needed to inform her older brother and her sister-in-law about the morning episodes at Pine Ridge.

She answered all her sister-in-law's questions as completely as possible and suggested they call Brother Dean if they wanted more clarification. "I'm so sorry Anthony needed to be part of this frightening morning. If I can be of any more help, please call me."

Ellen hung up the phone. Would this cultural turmoil and chaotic civil rights saga ever end?

CHAPTER ELEVEN

*I*t didn't take long for Brother Dean to lose his teaching contract at Riverdale High. But his reputation as an excellent teacher followed him. A neighboring high school hired him within weeks of his dismissal.

Dean requested the Sheriff's Department continue the investigation regarding the parsonage shooting. The burly local sheriff dismissed the incident with, "There is insufficient evidence to make any arrests, and we can't tell anything from measly bullet casings. As for the moonshine still, it happens. Just stay out of the woods." Case closed!

A balmy green autumn burrowed its way into a cold, wet winter. Violence quieted in the Missula and Pine Ridge areas. Many native white Mississippians watched in utter dismay as the Reverend Dr. Martin Luther King, Jr. organized the black South into peaceful Civil Rights marches under his banner, "A heart filled with love can conquer anything–even bigotry."

The Ku Klux Klan resorted to the opposite tactic. White land owners quaked in their black bottom-land boots. The KKK mushroomed their ranks by touting the fear tactic of "You will lose the shirt off your backs if you don't keep those lazy niggers and dirty Choctaws in their place. Their place right now is in your cotton fields."

Minorities who dared question the KKK's violent agenda, found their churches and homes going up in flames or worse yet, loved ones lynched. Mennonite farmers tried to steer clear of either extreme. Ellen wanted to believe Dr. King's message of nonviolence but the fear tactics of the KKK prompted her to drive with her doors locked and windows closed whenever driving alone.

But Christmas was in the air. Barry called Ellen. "Ellen, Pine Ridge Chapel has invited our youth group to join them for Christmas Caroling on Friday, December 24. Are you free to accompany us?"

"Oh, I love Christmas caroling! That will be delightful. Let me check my work schedule. Oh, no," she groaned. "I'm scheduled to work that night. I was already anticipating the great time we'd have. I feel like a balloon that has just been deflated. Sometimes being a night shift nursing supervisor yanks me back from the fun opportunities the rest of you have."

Barry chuckled, "You've got that right. We'll miss having you along, but I'll fill you in next week."

The combined Mennonite Youth Fellowships from Pine Ridge and Missula met at Pine Ridge on Christmas Eve. Barry pulled up beside the chapel. Teens spilled out of the van and into the Pine Ridge church bus with high fives. Their excitement was palpable.

Barry called to Brother Dean above the din of eager teenagers, "Let me re-park this van and I'll be with you shortly."

"That's fine. We'll wait," Dean replied.

Typically Barry parked the Missula van next to the church. Tonight something compelled him to re-park the vehicle near the road, next to the parking lot exit. He dismissed his intuition as a passing thought and joined the boisterous group on the bus. With Brother Dean at the wheel, the group of thirty youth drove off for a night of fun and fellowship.

The youth sang with abandon, rendering a Choctaw cadence to traditional Christmas carols. By nine p. m. they headed back toward the Ginders' for donuts and hot chocolate.

En-route to the chapel, Lacey, a bubbly fifteen-year-old shared. "When we were singing at Granny Tubby's, I was standing next to her as she sat in her old rocking chair. Granny gripped my hand and had tears in her eyes. I know she liked our singing."

Ben Rennie, the eighteen-year-old youth group president spoke with hesitation, "Yeah, and when we were leaving old Chief Tatum's house, he came out to the porch to shake my hand and said, 'Ya gogay (thank-you) Ben, for coming.' Can you imagine, Chief Tatum thanking me? I'm just a kid." Ben shook his head while staring at the palms of his hands as if they held the answer. Everyone knew Chief Tatum's quiet action was an affirmation of Ben's leadership, a rarity for one so young.

Within minutes, they rounded the last bend. Brother Dean guided the bus to a stop in the church parking lot. Thirty seconds of stunned silence ensued. Then screams and groans of incredulity erupted.

"No, no, no! They can't do this to us!" ricocheted within the bus.

Teens and staff poured out of the vehicle, surveying the devastation in muted anguish.

The walls of the Chapel sanctuary and Sunday school wing had exploded into a pile of rubble. Two fluorescent light fixtures dangled at crazy angles. The pulpit was charred, yet the intricate Choctaw cross on its front panel remained intact. The church archway stood as a beacon of hope even though the bomb had been placed at the front entrance. Concrete cracked like splintered glass, but the doors to the sanctuary stood. Paradoxes everywhere.

One page of a hymn book fluttered by in the brisk December breeze.

And the endless haunting questions began.

"Why? Why?"

"Why was Pine Ridge Chapel, a church known for its peace position, destroyed much like the seventy other Mississippi churches?"

Girls whisked away unbidden glistening tears with furtive hands. Guys maintained a stoic Choctaw jaw. By some internal signal, the group gathered again near the bus. Their need for security had been ripped apart with the bombing. In the secluded chapel location, the carolers and staff were the first to witness the crime scene.

"Now I understand," Barry commented in a dazed voice. "It was God's spirit that prompted me to park that van near the exit. Had it been in its usual spot, it too would have been destroyed."

Brother Dean nodded in assent.

Then he turned his attention to the group. "Do you still want to go to Dad and Mom Ginder's?"

The youth murmured their agreement. Brother Dean was amazed how in spite of their grief and fear of reprisals, the Choctaw teens did not want to be disrespectful of Mrs. Ginder who had prepared the anticipated late night snack for them. But their hearts were not in the hot chocolate and donuts, a treat they rarely had the opportunity to savor. Gone was the jovial spirit of an hour ago.

Except for an occasional whispered "thank you," the group silently filed through the buffet line, then congregated in the living room. It was Ben who found his voice first. "They've bombed our chapel, but they haven't destroyed our church," They still had each other.

Pastor Neal and Brother Dean stepped into the kitchen to notify Sheriff Robbins and his deputy, Clarence Parker, of the disaster. When they returned to the group, they were frowning.

"What's wrong?" Mrs. Ginder asked.

"Sheriff Robbins didn't sound that concerned," Pastor Neal said. "He told us he'd be out to take a look at nine a.m., two days after Christmas which won't be until Monday."

Brother Dean stared at Pastor Neal. "You don't suppose the Law had been forewarned of the bombing or possibly endorsed the perpetrators, do you?"

Pastor Neal shrugged, and the youth remained quiet until the pastors decided it would be best to get the kids home.

The ride back to Missula was shrouded in silence.

Chapter Twelve

The phone shattered the early morning quiet on Christmas Day as Ellen walked into her room at the Nurses' Residence. She wanted nothing more than sleep after a night of meeting relentless patient needs. An unusual sense of foreboding gripped her. Family and friends rarely called her at the end of the night shift. With reluctance, Ellen lifted the receiver.

"Hello, Ellen speaking." Her voice betrayed her reticence.

"Ellen, this is Brother Don. I wanted to call you before you heard the morning news. Are you all right?"

The hair on her arms and at the nape of her neck lifted. Why was he asking the question?

"I think I'm okay, but what's happening?" Her mind flitted in a hundred directions. Had someone from church or her family been injured? What would prompt her pastor to call her at seven-thirty in the morning on Christmas Day?

"Ellen, please sit down. I know you must be very tired from working all night." He paused. "We don't know why, but Pine Ridge Chapel was bombed last evening."

"Bombed? You mean as in destroyed?" Her voice escalated several decibels. The thought was incredulous.

"Essentially, yes. Very little of the Chapel will be salvageable. Brother Dean, Barry and the MYF carolers were the first to arrive at the scene."

Ellen moaned, slumping into a nearby chair. "What, why, how?" Questions burrowed their way into her consciousness and spilled out in rapid fire fashion.

Brother Don took a deep breath and began, "I'm not real comfortable discussing this by phone but meet us at the Millers Monday evening at seven p. m. In the meantime, try to get some sleep. I must tell you about Ben Rennie's remarkable assessment. He told the group, 'They've bombed our Chapel but they haven't destroyed our Church.'"

He sighed, then continued. "I would also suggest you not discuss this with anyone until an investigation can be done by the authorities. Ellen, will you be able to sleep?"

"How can I sleep when others are devastated? But thanks, Brother Don for letting me know. I'll cope. You can rest assured,

I will follow your suggestion." With that, Ellen let the receiver slide onto the phone.

She trudged to the bathroom to wash her face. Her eyes were heavy as she undressed and fell into bed. She let out a troubled sigh as she lay on her back and stared at the ceiling in her darkened room. Possible scenes of the bombed out chapel invaded her mind. Sleep eluded her for hours.

Eventually she fell into a fitful sleep. On Christmas evening Ellen joined her family for a subdued celebration. Sunday passed in a blur.

At seven p.m. Monday, the Choctaw Tribe, Pine Ridge attendees, and white mission staff from Pine Ridge and Missula converged in the tool shed of a sympathetic Mennonite farmer. No Choctaws dared enter the nearby community building.

The bombing demanded an answer. A segment of the typically peaceful band of the Mississippi Choctaw Nation was itching for a fight.

Ellen left her residence early so she could stop to see what was left of the Chapel. Nothing could have prepared her for the devastation that greeted her as she turned into the church parking lot. Yellow tape cordoned what had been a safe, secure house of worship five days ago. She felt propelled to get out of her car and move toward the yellow tape.

Oh, God. This looks like a war zone. Choking sobs gripped her as she surveyed the pile of rubble—a monument of man's inhumanity to man. Standing there alone did not feel safe, as though someone had invaded her personal quiet retreat. She felt violated and vulnerable.

What must all her Choctaw friends be feeling? Will's parents, Chief and Granny Tatum, were a part of the Pine Ridge Chapel congregation. Would Shonia feel as invaded as Ellen did at this moment?

When Ellen entered the Miller driveway, Brother Don walked rapidly toward her. His face was etched with concern as she slowed to a stop. Cars and vans lined the drive leading to the large pole shed that had been cleared of farm implements in preparation for tonight's meeting. Without any preliminaries, Brother Don opened the passenger door and slid into the seat beside her.

Seeing her tear-streaked face, he said, "You've been to the Chapel." Brother Don waited until she retrieved a tissue from her purse. "I wanted to speak to you privately since we don't know who may be listening. We think the bombing may be in retaliation of Brother Neal's family being sympathetic of the murdered Civil Rights Workers. Or it could be due to the Mennonite stance of non-discrimination. We're guessing it may also be because our Choctaw sisters who have become Christians are no longer willing to serve as mistresses for the white men's lust.

"Whatever the motivation may be for the bombing, be very cautious as to what you say on the phone. All our phone lines may be tapped by the Klan. Be careful. No one from the Chapel or Missula has participated in Civil Rights activities but the Klan may not come to the same conclusion."

"I understand," Ellen said. Would she be a Klan suspect too? She gripped the steering wheel.

Brother Don continued, "When Sheriff Robbins and Deputy Parker came out this morning to conduct an investigation of the bombing, they were laughing as though it were some strange joke carried out by pranksters.

Tonight Chief Tatum has given us no clue as to what he will say to his people. But we do know there is an undercurrent of anger among the younger warriors. Pray Ellen. We don't need any more violence."

Ellen had prayed for the protective power of God during the cross burning episode and she firmly believed God delivered her. Would he choose to over-ride the evil intent of those responsible for the bombing by displaying his protection for the people of Pine Ridge Chapel? Ellen prayed it would be so.

Brother Neal, being the senior pastor, opened the meeting with prayer. "Lord, give us hearts of peace and not of violence.

Help each of us to think clearly in this hour of crisis, in Jesus' name, Amen."

Chief Tatum rose to his towering six-foot height in full Choctaw regalia. His leathery arms crossed his broad chest encased in a bright blue tribal shirt with its intricate appliquéd white triangles creating an impressive border across the front and back yoke. A four-inch- wide beaded Choctaw necklace completed Chief's garb.

Ellen was sure she had never seen the Chief so regal.

This would be a tribal moment and the chief was here to lead his people. Deep wrinkles in his weathered olive face lent an aura of wisdom. Chief's black eyes pierced the crowd. An instant hush descended.

He spoke with dignity. "You know the story of our Nation. On September 27, 1830, our fathers signed the Treaty of Dancing Rabbit Creek. We were displaced from our ancestral lands by white man. On the night before Christmas, white man bombed our Chapel. Will we go on the warpath, or will we choose the path of peace as taught by our Lord and our pastors? You warriors want revenge and rightfully so."

Ellen shivered as muttered guttural assents emanated from a significant number of Choctaw men. Across the barnlike building, Ellen's eyes met Shonia's fear-laced gaze. Shonia would have overheard talk in Chief Tatum's household. What did she know that Ellen didn't know? Would there be more destruction and possibly bloodshed? Ellen determined she would find a way to connect with Shonia tonight.

In centuries-old Choctaw style, the Chief chose to demonstrate what he was about to say. "Will, would you come up here for a moment?"

Standing eye to eye with his son, the chief extended his right hand. "Will, put your right hand up against mine." As Will's hand met the chief's open palm, Will felt a push against his hand. Instinctively, Will pushed back.

Chief Tatum asked, "Son, what were my instructions to you?"

"You said to put my hand against yours, but you pushed." Will's dark skin reddened.

Chief turned to the group. "You see, when I pressed against Will's hand, he naturally pushed back. Three days ago, we were pushed by violence against our Choctaw Nation. Tonight, we can choose to meet force with force and be met with more force. But I would like you, my people, to consider a different way. Think about what one of our wise young warriors said after surveying the rubble. He said, 'They've bombed our Chapel, but they haven't destroyed our Church.' We can either choose to rebuild or plot revenge."

No one spoke for quite a few moments.

CHAPTER THIRTEEN

*E*llen sensed an amazing change in the tense atmosphere of the crowd. Ben's words, *They've bombed our Chapel, but they haven't destroyed our Church,* reverberated in the silence.

Then a noiseless phenomenon occurred. Beginning with the eldest warrior to the youngest teenager, men stood, crossed their arms and silently formed a line originating on either side of their chief and encircling the assembly. Without a word, the men declared they were standing with the Chief.

Ellen's tears threatened to spill down her cheeks. Choctaw women looked at the floor to keep their emotions under control. They were taught from when they were little girls never to embarrass their husbands, fathers, or brothers with public tears.

Chief Tatum stepped forward. "My people have spoken. Brother Neal, Brother Don, and Brother Dean, would you come and tells us how we can begin to rebuild?"

Brother Neal's voice trembled with emotion. "You men have chosen to show the world that love is stronger than hate. Brother Don, I believe you are familiar with how the broader church might be of help in our hour of need."

Don's face was alight with his passion. "You have been wronged and suffered great loss. The rest of the church body hurts with you. But I have good news. Out of the rubble and ashes, hope will rise as we work together.

Don't forget, you are part of a larger church body! Two hours ago, the director of the Ohio unit of Mennonite Disaster Service called to ask if they could help. That means MDS would send men and resources to work with us. What do you say men? Shall we call our church brothers to help us?"

Tribal decorum evaporated. Calls of, "bring'em on", and "I can help tomorrow," and "I'll be here after work," came from the tight circle of men.

Brother Dean quickly grabbed a clipboard and inserted a sign-up sheet. For the illiterate, he filled in their names and times when they would be available to help. What had been a gathering of fear and anger and doom turned into an evolving current of possibility and celebration.

Brother Don slipped out of the meeting to call Ohio while Ellen made her way across the tool shed to Shonia. "Hello Shonia, I've missed you a lot."

This time the young Choctaw mother did not avoid her. Shonia whispered, "Come outside with me." Abandoning Choctaw mores, she threw her arms around Ellen in a lingering hug. Silently, their tears mingled; tears of grief, tears of relief, tears of loneliness, tears because of needing to give up a dream.

Fearing unseen eyes and ears, Ellen asked in a hushed tone, "Would you be comfortable going to my car to talk?"

Shonia nodded, her eyes scanning the shadows.

Once sheltered in the relative safety of the car, the story unfolded. "So sorry, Ellen. Can't do English lessons. Boss-man says to quit or he make me to do bad things again. When I see burning cross, I know the boss-man with KKK. I afraid for you and my family.

If I not in field, boss-man say no *shkullie*—money. When no *shkullie*, have no food, no clothes, no house, no job. I dreamed if I read, I teach Will to read. Then we stop chopping cotton. Ellen, will this never end?" Shonia's voice trailed into a low-pitched wail.

Ellen laid a gentle hand on her friend's shoulder. "Shonia, right now I don't know the answer to all the injustice you are suffering. But I do know that God cares and He weeps with us. The warriors have said they will rebuild. They refuse to be intimidated. We will walk through this hard time with you and your people. We can pray for God's protection for each other. We are all part of the Body of Christ. Remember Ben's words. Something good will come out of all this mess. I don't know what it is, but I can see it coming."

The two friends prayed together that God's protection would encircle them and everyone associated with Pine Ridge and Missula. Soon, they made their way back to Farmer Miller's implement shed, lest their absence from the group became too noticeable. Mr. Miller agreed to make the shed available for Sunday morning services while the rebuilding was in progress. Space heaters would be used to make the building more comfortable in the midst of cold, wintery winds.

The crowd was ready to exit when Brother Don reappeared. "Listen, my friends. I've spoken to the director of the Ohio Mennonite Disaster Service. He will be flying down tomorrow. Men and equipment should be arriving within thirty-six hours. In the meantime, whoever is available to work, meet us at the Chapel tomorrow morning at nine a. m. to begin the clean-up process. Now, let's all go home and get some sleep."

CHAPTER FOURTEEN

*S*leep sounded like a welcome relief after the evening stressors. But it would need to wait. Ellen was scheduled to supervise another shift of night duty. An hour later, she stepped into the nurse's station to receive evening Report from her dorm mate, Anne Maria. The list contained the usual pre-and-post-operative patients needing follow-up and early morning lab work. Medical patients in the white and black halls would need monitoring, especially those receiving intravenous fluids.

With Report concluded, Anne Maria asked to see Ellen in the nurse's office. Behind a firmly closed door, Anna Marie began. "Remember, last month's mission staff meeting? Brother Don told us about this teenage Choctaw girl, Rena Westin, who was raped by a drunken black man at a Choctaw funeral cry—you know, an all-night wake—out at Bogue Chito? I've never been to a Choctaw cry, but I understand there is a lot of feasting and drinking that occurs, and Rena was abducted."

Ellen nodded. "I remember Brother Don indicated that Rena's family didn't want to accept this child of mixed Choctaw-black blood and rejected Rena in the process. So, Brother Don found a Mennonite family, the Hershbergers, to care for her during her pregnancy. Is she about to deliver?"

"Yes. In fact, Mrs. Hershberger called an hour ago to say Rena is in the early stages of labor and may come in on your shift."

"I hope she does come in tonight. Rena has gone through so much trauma. If she comes in on the day shift, we can be sure our Director of Nurses, Mrs. Jacobs, will put her in the open ward on the black side. That will give her no privacy and the very real possibility of being harassed by other patients. Who is her physician?"

"Dr. Percy has done all her pre-natal care and is on-call tonight. I'll be praying for Rena and for y'all as a medical team."

"Thanks, Anne Maria. I appreciate your prayers. I'll make sure Rena is well cared-for if she comes in as an OB admission within the next eight hours."

Anne Maria waved her greetings from the door. "Have a good night."

Ellen sat at the desk tapping her pen for a few moments before making rounds. If Rena goes into hard labor on my shift I wonder what the D.O.N. will say if I put her on the white hall? I have an uneasy feeling it won't be pretty.

The night held few quiet moments as Ellen and her staff attempted to meet the needs of each patient in the fifty-bed hospital. At five-thirty a. m. she sat down to chart patient progress notes, only to be propelled into action by the Emergency Room buzzer.

Sprinting toward the ER Ellen prayed, *Lord, let it be Rena, but You also know I don't have time right now to assist with a delivery. Whatever is on the other side of the ER door, I know you will give me the wisdom to deal with it.*

Approaching the outer doors, Ellen came face-to-face with Rena and Mr. and Mrs. Hershberger. Rena was obviously having contractions which she bore without emitting a sound.

Mrs. Hershberger explained the birth pains were coming every five minutes.

Ellen eased Rena into a wheelchair with a gentle hand. Stopping at the ER Nurse's station, she took the time to place a call to Dr. Percy.

The physician picked up the phone on the first ring.

"Dr. Percy, this is Ms. Yoder at Missula General. Your patient Rena Westin has just arrived and is in obvious labor. Where shall I admit her? The hospital is crowded tonight. We have room one which is a private room or room ten which is semiprivate on the white hall, or bed thirty-eight on the black open ward." Rena didn't fit the usual categories of white or black.

Without hesitation, Dr. Percy instructed, "Take her to room one. I'll be in to check her in a few minutes."

Ellen licked her dry lips. She had an uneasy feeling there could be repercussions.

Dr. Percy came striding into room one within minutes of Rena's admission. "Rena, you've done a great job throughout this pregnancy. Now breathe deeply as I do the examination. We're here to help you through the tough part." His voice and touch were gentle.

Dr. Percy's soothing, reassuring voice calmed her and the terror in her eyes lessened. Rena's labor progressed with abrupt intensity. She moaned.

The doctor looked at Ellen and ordered, "Let's go!"

Minutes later, Rena lay on the delivery table. Doctor and nurse worked together in sync. By six-fifteen a. m. Rena delivered a beautiful, healthy, dark-olive skinned baby girl with lots of straight black hair. One minute the teenaged mother was laughing. The next minute she was crying as she cradled her baby in her arms for a few treasured moments.

Rena had already made the decision to release the child for adoption. Sobbing, she handed the baby back to Ellen who wept with her. Hospital policy dictated that once the baby entered the nursery, the biological mother would not be allowed to see or touch the infant again. The Hershbergers had assisted Rena in finding an out-of-state, childless Mennonite couple who would love and care for her baby. Rena didn't know the names or location of the couple since most adoptions in Mississippi were closed adoptions.

Ellen asked her LPN and nurse's aide to transfer Rena to room one while she carried Baby Westin to the nursery. The only department of Missula General that was integrated was the infant nursery. During sporadic quiet moments throughout the hospital, Ellen loved to slip into the nursery to hold an infant. No one chastised her for cradling a crying black or white child in her arms or for changing a diaper. Ina, the night shift cook-housekeeper-nursery worker, considered Ellen a God-send, particularly when three or more infants needed simultaneous attention.

Releasing the baby into Ina's ample arms, Ellen instructed, "Ina, Baby Westin is not to go out for feeding times. We will follow Dr. Percy's orders regarding formula. Take good care of her. She's precious."

Ina laughed. "You sez that 'bout ever' youngin' that comes in hea."

"You're right, Ina." Ellen chuckled. "Every infant is precious because they are a gift straight from God."

"I be carin' fo this 'un fo you, Ms. Ellen."

"Thank you, Ina."

Ellen retreated to the nurses' station, working frantically to prepare the morning Report for the day shift. True to form, the

Director of Nurses, Mrs. Jacobs walked into the station promptly at six-forty-five a. m. Her Assistant Director of Nurses, Betsy Hollis followed suit. Within minutes the station was buzzing with twelve members of the day nursing staff.

Mrs. Jacobs picked up the patient and nursery list. "Hmm, you must have had a delivery. Who is this Ms. Westin and why is she in room one?"

Ellen turned to the group. "Let's begin Report and I'll give you an update on each patient. Room one is Ms. Westin, a brave sixteen-year-old Choctaw girl who delivered a baby girl at six-fifteen this morning--"

"You mean you put a dirty Choctaw in one of our private rooms! What were you thinking, girl?" Ms. Hollis' attack reeked with disdain.

"I followed Dr. Percy's orders." Ellen should have been prepared for the fire storm, but the venom with which the head nurse spewed her accusations shocked her.

"As the Night Supervisor you could have suggested another room," Mrs. Jacobs spat out. "You Yankee nigger lovers think you can come down here and turn our world up-side-down. Well finish your report, girl, and we'll move this Ms. Westin to bed thirty-eight in the ward."

Ellen's head swam in the midst of the volatile onslaught. *Lord, keep me calm.* "It is my understanding that we cannot execute a patient transfer without a doctor's order."

Dr. Percy appeared at the Nurses' Station entrance unannounced. "Ms. Yoder's understanding of hospital protocol is correct. Out of all due respect for your concern, Ms. Jacobs, my obstetric patient, Ms. Rena Westin, whom I have seen for all her prenatal care, will remain in room one until I am confident that she is ready for discharge. She meets your criteria of wanting to admit primarily clean, infection-free patients. Reports of her progress are to be given to her foster family, Mr. & Mrs. Hershberger. It will be to your advantage to give her excellent care in preparation for her discharge. Now may I have Ms. Westin's chart to record my progress notes?"

Ms. Hollis handed Dr. Percy the chart.

The hostility in the Nurses' Station was so thick, it could be cut with a knife. Somehow Ellen completed the rest of Report. Stopping by briefly at room one, she noted Rena was asleep, no doubt physically and emotionally exhausted.

Mrs. Hershberger, sat at her bedside and looked up from reading.

Ellen put her finger to her lips and left the room.

She would have promised to check in on Rena when she returned to work at eleven p.m. but she couldn't be certain she would ever be allowed to set foot in the hospital again.

CHAPTER FIFTEEN

Stumbling into her room in the nurses' residence, Ellen quietly closed her door and flung herself onto the bed. Sobs of fear and frustration ripped from her inner being. She attempted to muffle her cries in the pillow. She didn't need an audience.

Lord, You said, "You know the way that I take and when you've tested me, I'll come forth as gold." Silver or even pewter would be just fine about now!

Ellen didn't know how long she laid there in her darkened, shade-drawn room. She finally slipped out of her wrinkled uniform and returned to bed. She drifted in and out of a restless twilight zone, sleeping in snatches.

Suddenly, the phone interrupted her troubled sleep. "Hello, this is Ellen."

"Hello Ms. Yoder. This is Mr. Landamann. I apologize if I am awakening you."

Ellen jerked into an upright position. Glancing at the clock, she blinked away her sleep-blurred vision. It was three p. m., her usual wake-up time. She had been too distraught to set an alarm.

This call was from the hospital CEO and would probably culminate in her exit interview. "Ms. Yoder, I understand you had a very stressful night. I would like to discuss with you the issues at hand," Mr. Landamann said. "Would you be free to come back to the hospital for an appointment in about an hour?"

Ellen swallowed hard to keep from choking. "Yes, sir, I can be there by four p. m."

Mr. Landamann bid her adieu and Ellen sprang into action. While showering and preparing for the interview, her thoughts threatened to spin out of control. It was Mr. Landamann that contacted Rosedale Mennonite Missions to request that I be recruited. Now he's probably regretting his appeal. Lord, give me the grace to accept being dismissed from the position where I thought you wanted me to serve. I was sure I was doing what you would have done last night but I feel like a total failure. I'm scared!

Four p.m. came. Ellen walked around the front of the hospital and into the stately, rounded dome entrance. She could have taken the shortcut through the patient wing but she had no desire to be accosted by the nursing hierarchy.

The CEO's administrative assistant ushered her into the plush oval office next to the rotunda. Mr. Landamann unfolded his lanky frame from the deep recesses of his leather-bound desk chair. He reminded Ellen of a gentle giant who could be kind, yet firm, while keeping an eagle-eye on hospital policy, staffing, and finances.

He leaned across the executive desk to shake her hand. "Please Ms. Yoder, have a seat and make yourself comfortable. I'm sure the past ten to eleven hours have been highly uncomfortable for you, just as they have been for all of us."

Ellen nodded, not trusting herself to speak or even daring to look up. *Please, Lord, let's get this over with. If he's going to fire me, I don't need a racist sermon.*

"Ms. Yoder, I want you to know the hospital is standing behind Dr. Percy's and your decision to integrate the hospital last night."

Had she heard correctly? Just in case, she quickly worked to remove any element of surprise from her face.

"I'm sure you are also aware Missula General's financial survival is partially dependent upon governmental subsidies. The new Medicaid policies state we must integrate the hospital if we wish to continue receiving reimbursement for our services."

For a split second she stopped breathing. What was he saying? Was Missula General reversing its century-old policies and procedures that were steeped in the very fabric of southern culture? Segregation practices in this southern town were as immovable as a granite mountain.

Ellen stole a surreptitious glance in Mr. Landamann's direction. Was he serious?

Looking very solemn, Mr. Landamann continued, "To say the least, I have been agonizing for months as to how we were going to accomplish integration without being tarred and feathered right out of town. You, Ms. Yoder, and Dr. Percy instituted the first step toward integration as of five-thirty this morning when you admitted Ms. Westin into room one. Allow me to congratulate you for your courage." Rising from his chair he reached out to shake Ellen's hand.

Releasing a long pent-up sigh, Ellen finally found her voice. "Thank you, Mr. Landamann. But allow me to be very honest with you. When I suggested room one to Dr. Percy, I wasn't thinking about Medicaid guidelines. My primary concern was for Ms. Westin's health and protection no matter what the consequences might be. I'm not here as a civil rights activist. I'm here to extend the love of Jesus to whoever might be entrusted to my care, even though that may cost me my position here at Missula General."

Ellen still braced herself for an inevitable dismissal. She had been so convinced she would be dismissed, that the full weight of what Mr. Landamann said hadn't fully registered.

A momentary smile flitted across the CEO's angular face as he leaned back into his king-sized chair. "Ms. Yoder, have you considered returning to school for a B. S. N?"

She shook her head, bewildered. "A Bachelor's in Nursing? No sir! As you know, I've just earned my R. N. I thought I would work several years before even considering a return to academia."

Was this his kind way of easing her out of her position without marring her record by firing her? The CEO seemed to be going on a rabbit trail that made no sense.

"Ms. Yoder, Medicaid specifies that hospitals not only comply with integration, but they must also employ a Director of Nurses who has achieved a Bachelor of Science in Nursing. Ms. Jacobs tells me she plans to retire within the next few years. Neither she, nor any of the current nurses who might qualify for the directorship have a B. S. N. You have demonstrated professional excellence, supervisory skills and integrity—all leadership essentials that I look for in a future nursing director.

"So my question remains. Ms. Yoder, would you consider returning to college for a bachelor's degree which would qualify you for the directorship here at Missula General?"

"I—I don't know, Mr. Landamann." Ellen's vocal chords weren't cooperating and her thoughts and her emotions were reeling. "I would like some time to think and pray about your proposal." Was he actually accepting rather than rejecting her and even offering a future promotion?

"That's fine, Ms. Yoder. Take some time to explore your options. Then check back with me in a few weeks. It's worth pursuing." He rose to shake her hand and bid her good day.

Ellen left the office, uncertain whether to dance into the late afternoon shadows or to conclude Mr. Landamann's offer was totally absurd. By now she was wide-awake and rejuvenated.

CHAPTER SIXTEEN

*E*llen's mental barrage of questions buckled her into an emotional roller coaster. She thoroughly enjoyed school with its academic challenges and she had graduated near the top echelon of her class. But how could she finance such a venture? After three consecutive years in nursing school, her financial reserves were exhausted. The monthly two-hundred-dollar stipend from Missula General had done little more than sustain her basic needs.

As a twenty-two-year old, she wouldn't even consider asking her parents for assistance. Her parents had sacrificed significant income to follow their own call of God to come to Missula.

Lord, you know my unspoken dream is to become a wife and mother. I know it's important to pursue my calling as a nurse but I never intended to invest my whole life in a career.

Coming to Mississippi had not inched her any closer to her long-term dream. Socially, the Missula community and church held few possibilities for her. Barry and Dixon were both attached to lovely girls from their home communities. Ellen had casually dated several local young men but they seemed intimidated by her R.N. Missula's Mennonite farming community embraced a certain uneasiness regarding higher education. There were times when Ellen felt the need to filter part of her professional vocabulary, lest her peers think she was "putting on airs." Would a B. S. N. widen the cultural gap and push her dream into total oblivion?

Ellen's immediate impulse was to share the news of Mr. Landamann's offer with Anne Maria, but she was on duty. Grabbing her purse and car keys, Ellen eased the silver Bug onto Main Street, lined with magnolia trees. She had to share this with Pop and Mom.

Driving a straight-stick had become second nature. Ellen cruised through town, unmindful of the elegant southern mansions lining both sides of the street. Upon her initial arrival in Mississippi, she had been awed by the magnificence of the Ferral estate with its quartet of towering white pillars framing the ornate front entrance. Curved scrolls graced the top of each colonial pillar.

Several weeks ago, a black domestic ushered Ellen and her father into the grandeur of the Ferral's front hall, dominated by a highly polished winding, wooden staircase. Mr. Yoder was a master craftsman known locally and in surrounding urban areas for his skill and integrity. They were delivering a restored love seat to Mrs. Ferral.

Ellen envisioned a southern belle with a hooped skirt attempting to seat herself next to her suitor on the cranberry brocade of the tufted loveseat with its intricate rose carvings in the black walnut trim. Today, the allure of a bygone era simply blended into a familiar part of the landscape.

Missula's Courthouse with its eight stately Greek columns and brick Federal architecture cast its afternoon shadow on surrounding storefronts built in the early 1900s. Ellen drove between cars parked on an angel on both sides of Main Street. Her mind was not on the quaint old town atmosphere. *Lord, where do you want me to go from here and what do you want me to do? You've promised you would show me the way.*

She knew Mom and Pop wouldn't mind an unannounced visit during the dinner hour. As she entered the door, Poppa glanced up from reading the Grit newspaper. "Well, well, here comes *de glennie,* my little, Betsy."

Ellen permitted no one but her father to call her Betsy; his pet name for his youngest daughter. She suspected she would forever be his *glennie* Betsy. Without doubt, she could count on the wisdom and protection of her father. Today that felt like a soothing balm in the midst of her churning emotions.

Mom called from the kitchen. "You will join us for dinner, won't you, Ellen? We're having pecan pie for dessert."

"Mom, you know that's my favorite. I'll be happy to join you if it's not too inconvenient."

"Inconvenient? Having our children join us for a meal is never inconvenient! It's a privilege. Come, let's sit down to eat." Francis Yoder had a heart that was bigger than her dining room table which could extend to seat twelve or more at a moment's notice. Being Mrs. Hospitality came as natural as breathing.

Daniel Yoder bowed his head. "Father we thank you for this meal, lovingly prepared by Mother. Thank you for Ellen's surprise visit in the midst of her busy schedule. We praise you for what you have done, and will do, in the lives of each of our loved ones. In Jesus name I pray. Amen."

Daniel reached for the plate of fresh homemade bread and passed it to Ellen. "Now tell us what brings you here in the middle of the week." His eyes twinkled with anticipation.

"Pop and Mom, you'll never believe what happened during the past twenty-four hours." Ellen reiterated as clearly as possible the admission of Rena Westin to room one, the birth of Rena's baby, and the explosive nurses' report that followed. She mentioned Dr. Percy's directives to Ms. Jacobs and the hostility she experienced from her co-workers. When sharing how she had cried herself to sleep, Mom's eyes filled with compassionate tears. She reached out to squeeze Ellen's hand.

"But Mom and Pop, at three this afternoon Mr. Landamann called me, asking that I come in for a four p. m. appointment."

"Mr. Landamann?" Pop queried as his thick eyebrows lifted. Mr. Yoder was a handsome gentleman with jet black hair. Most folks had no clue he'd passed his sixty-fifth birthday.

"Yes. That's why I need the help of both of you to sort out what I should do next. I went into the meeting, certain I'd be fired from my position at Missula General. I assumed I wouldn't be allowed to set foot in the hospital again and would need to move out of the nurses' residence."

Her mother clasped her hand to her chest and sucked in a quick breath.

In a carefully controlled tone, Daniel asked, "What did Mr. Landamann say?"

"An amazing thing happened. Mr. Landamann told me the hospital would stand behind Dr. Percy's and my decision to place a Choctaw in room one. He went on to thank me for starting the integration process because Medicaid policies demand hospitals comply with integration or their federal funds will be cut. Missula General can't survive financially without Medicaid reimbursement."

Daniel shook his head, trying to understand the sudden turn of events. "This is almost beyond my imagination, that my little

Betsy would be integrating Missula General. What else did the hospital administrator have to say?"

"Well, according to Mr. Landamann, Medicaid also requires hospitals to hire a Director of Nurses' who has a B. S. N. Ms. Jacobs plans to retire in the next few years. So he asked if I would consider returning to college for a Bachelor's degree. The D.O.N.'s position would be an option for me if I decided to return to Missula General. He's sure I have leadership capabilities. I'm not so sure I could be an effective Yankee nursing director in Confederate territory. But I wonder—should I try?"

Her parents' eyes met. Ellen glimpsed a combination of shock and concern. Mom Yoder's voice was tentative. "What did you tell Mr. Landamann?"

Ellen couldn't decipher whether she was sensing a hint of pride or a dose of caution or both in her mother's question. "I didn't know what to say. I told him I needed time to pray about it."

"That's an excellent place to begin." Pop affirmed. He was never one to impulsively jump into a situation. "We'll pray with you, Ellen. What do you think life would be like as a student again? After three intense years of school, you've had a taste of freedom from studies."

"You're right, Pop. I was tired of being a student when I came almost a year ago. But I do enjoy the challenge of academia. It would give me the tools I need to become a better nurse coordinator. However, returning to campus would mean two more years of living on a financial shoestring. I'm not sure how I could finance it." Ellen toyed with the food on her plate.

"If the Lord wants you back in school, the finances will come." Her father had lived through enough financial crises to firmly believe in God's provision.

"Have you thought about what college you would like to attend?" Mom asked.

Ellen half-expected her to say, *Please don't leave us so soon, Ellen*. But Daniel and Francis Yoder had made a commitment never to interfere with what might be God's will for their seven sons and four daughters.

"The only school I feel comfortable applying to, is Eastern Mennonite College in Harrisonburg, Virginia. Not long ago I received one of their mailings describing a new Bachelor of Science program designed specifically for registered nurses. Thinking I might check into it in two or three years, I filed it. Now I wonder if God's spirit was tapping me on the shoulder and I didn't recognize it."

"While Mother and I would like to keep you nearby, this may be God prompting you to take your next giant step of faith." Daniel took another bite of savory meatloaf.

"Maybe, but for admission into the next semester, I should have been applying last November. I have no clue as to whether E. M. C. would even have an opening this late in the academic year. We're nearing the end of May. God will need to open doors very quickly if I am to attend the fall semester which is only three months away." Ellen looked at the food she had forgotten to eat. She shrugged. Just thinking about all the steps she would need to take in order to arrive on campus by fall seemed overwhelming.

Mom turned to her daughter. "Did Mr. Landamann say anything about the need to sign a contract?"

"No, he didn't. I don't think they would ask me to sign a contract unless Missula General would be willing and able to pay for my education. I can't imagine the hospital has funds to make such an offer."

Mom nodded in agreement then asked, "What if you meet a young man on campus and you decide to get married? What if he's not interested or doesn't feel called to return to Mississippi? Then what?"

"Hmm. I haven't had time to think of those possibilities. Since I know no one on campus, it seems like a remote probability."

Her parents exchanged knowing grins.

"I guess I'll cross that bridge, if or when, I get to it." The idea posed by her mother was an intriguing one. Ellen tucked it away for future reference. For now, she had lots of other "what ifs" to consider. What if her application would be rejected for some unknown reason. What if there would be no available scholarship funds. Ellen's academic scores would not block her entrance but the lack of money could.

Daniel Yoder suggested they join hands as he began to intercede for his daughter, "Lord, you know Ellen's need and possible opportunity to pursue her B. S. N. If it is your will that she attend Eastern Mennonite, I pray for open doors. If this is the direction you want her to take, give her the assurance that you've already stepped into her tomorrow. In Jesus' name I pray, Amen."

Ellen blinked away tears of gratitude for parents whose faith was big enough for all three of them. She felt encircled in their love. "Thanks, Pop and Mom. I was sure I could count on your help in sorting out this whole situation. Thanks for your listening ear and your support. Now I know what I need to do." She finished her pecan pie in short order.

Ellen wished her parents a "goodnight" and covered the five miles to the nurses' residence in record time.

CHAPTER SEVENTEEN

*E*xcept for the soft glow of the foyer table lamp, the Nurses' Residence was dark when Ellen returned. Her five housemates must either be out for the evening or working. Tonight she didn't want to spend time stopping to say, "Hey y'all. How was your day?"

Feeling wide-awake, she unlocked the door of her room. She was on a mission and headed straight for her consignment shop, no-frills desk. This utilitarian bit of furniture had three, four-inch-deep drawers on the right half of the pint-sized faux wood desk top. Ellen knew precisely where she had filed the Eastern Mennonite College brochure. She lifted the mailing from the bottom drawer and glanced around her small domain with a wry grin. At least these cozy quarters forced her to remain organized.

Taking a quick look at the clock, she calculated she had a bit of time to slip the application form into her manual typewriter. If she hurried, she might even have time to complete the requested information before preparing to return to work at eleven o'clock. Above the cadence of clicking typewriter keys Ellen mused, *What am I doing? Is this real? Twenty-four hours ago I wasn't even considering a return to the academic world. What will the Mission Board think of this turn of events? What about Shonia? And will there be any scholarships available at this late date?*

Ellen filled in the last blank several hours later and signed the final signature line. She straightened her cramped shoulders and massaged stiff neck muscles. She recalled that her high school guidance counselor had encouraged all seniors to request several official transcripts of their grades for future job or college applications. Tonight she was grateful she had followed his advice and also obtained additional copies of her nursing school transcripts. Including them with her application to E.M.C. would expedite the process.

Now it was time to go back to work and "face the music."

The light was still on in room one when Ellen made rounds at eleven thirty p.m. With a gentle knock she slipped into the room.

Rena was sitting in the leather bedside chair; her face awash with tears.

"Rena, are you hurting?'

She nodded. "Here." She gestured toward her empty arms. "Not here." She indicated her flattened stomach.

Ellen dropped to her knees beside the chair and put her arms around the shoulders of the teenage mother. Leaning into the nurse's shoulder, Rena began to cry great heaving sobs rising from the depths of her being. Ellen suspected much of the pain of the past nine months, plus the trauma of relinquishing the infant with whom she had bonded, was overwhelming Rena.

Ellen cradled her, handing her tissues until the sobbing quieted. She spoke gently. "Rena, you know I can't bring the baby to you, but I will hold her for you and tell her again and again that you love her. Even babies understand the word *love*. You can send her to her adoptive Mommy and Daddy, knowing that she was loved and not rejected by her biological mother. Would you like to give her a name?"

For the first time, a glimmer of peace settled over Rena. "Yes! Yes I would like to name her, Marie Ellen Westin, for the two kindest women I know. Maybe she'll grow up to be like you and Marie." It was an unusual declaration for one as reserved as Rena.

Now it was Ellen's turn to grab the nearby box of tissues. "Rena, I am deeply honored. I'm sure your housemother, Marie, will feel honored as well. You've had a long day. Would you like me to bring you some medication to help you sleep, which will also help you regain your strength?"

Rena nodded.

Ellen strode to the nurses' station, returning promptly with the medication Dr. Percy had prescribed. Switching off the bedside light, Ellen said, "Goodnight Rena. Call me if you need me. I'm not far away."

"Goodnight, Ms Ellen. I'll be okay."

Throughout the night, Ellen took every available opportunity to hold baby Marie Ellen. Her time with the infant would be curtailed. Nestling the baby's cheek against her own, she marveled at the soft delicate creation within her arms. She was startled by the instinctive maternal love rising unbidden within her as she murmured over and over, "Marie Ellen, your Momma Rena, loves you. Your Momma Rena loves you."

Ellen hoped she too would someday cuddle her own infant in her arms but under very different circumstances.

CHAPTER EIGHTEEN

T he night had wings. At the stroke of six a. m. Dr. Percy appeared at the nurses' station. "Good morning, Ms. Yoder. How is my patient in room one?"

Ellen was surprised to see the doctor so early since his usual hour for making patient rounds was eight o'clock. "Ms. Westin had a rocky start at the beginning of this shift. Here are my nurse's notes that highlight how I found her. The medication you prescribed helped her sleep the rest of the night."

She handed Rena's chart to the doctor. Reading her cryptic notes couched in words to protect Rena from further discrimination, the physician nodded as he read. "Thanks. Thanks Ms. Yoder, for being here when my patient was distressed. Let's go see if she's ready for discharge."

Ms. Westin's luxurious black hair framed her pensive face as she greeted the medical team. Dr. Percy did a thorough physical exam before broaching the question, "Ms. Westin would you like to go home with the Hershbergers today? Physically you are doing very well. I can write the order so you can leave at eight o'clock this morning. If you run into any difficulty whatsoever, you can call me. The adoptive parents are due to arrive at ten."

"If I leave early, will my baby be alright?" Fear laced Rena's eyes. Even though she had not seen baby Marie Ellen since the delivery, it seemed Rena believed her presence in the hospital formed an invisible shield of protection around her child.

Taking Rena's hand, Ellen asked, "Rena, would you be more comfortable if I came back at ten o'clock to meet the adoptive parents and make sure baby Marie leaves safely in the arms of her new family?"

Ellen omitted the baby's middle name, feeling too self-conscious in the doctor's presence to admit a newborn had been named in her honor.

Tears trickled down Rena's face. Her speech was just above a whisper. "I'd like that. Thank you, Ms. Ellen."

Ellen fell in step with the doctor as he headed toward the nurses' station to write discharge orders. "Isn't it a bit early for discharge?" she asked. It had only been forty-eight hours since the delivery and post-partum patients were rarely discharged before seventy-two.

Dr. Percy slowed his stride. "I agree. It is early, Ms. Yoder. However, I think it is in our patient's best interest to be discharged from this hostile environment. I detect no medical reason to prolong her hospital stay. Marie Hershberger will help Ms. Westin with any follow-up orders, plus provide the emotional support she needs. Rena doesn't need any harsh words from hospital staff who may not understand her plight.

I want you to know that I appreciate your willingness to come back to assist in the baby's transfer when you could be sleeping at that hour."

"You're welcome, Dr. Percy." Ellen's voice trembled. She looked out the window to hide tears welling behind her eyelids. Had she volunteered to return for Rena's sake? Or was she helping with the transfer because she needed to say goodbye to the baby who had encircled her heart? She decided both were true.

For the past eight hours Ellen had been dreading Report at the close of the night shift. She steeled herself for whatever was coming. She began, "In room one Ms. Westin—"

"She is not Ms. Westin," the assistant director, Ms. Hollis, who was receiving Report snorted. "The patient is Rena!"

Ellen ignored the ethnic slur and continued. "Dr. Percy, is discharging Ms. Westin at eight a. m. The Hershbergers will be here soon. Baby Westin is scheduled to be released to the adoptive parents at ten this morning."

"Good riddance," someone echoed.

The night supervisor felt it best to avoid giving credence to any racial insinuations and continued the rest of Report without incident.

Thirty minutes before the designated hour, Ellen entered the newborn nursery. The nurse's aide was busy tending crying babies. Marie added her tiny whimper to the chorus. Ellen deftly changed her diaper and warmed some formula.

The aide exclaimed, "Thank ya, Jesus, fo Ms. Ellen."

Choosing an inviting rocking chair, Ellen rocked the tiny one and sang a lullaby. Baby Marie drank like a hungry little kitten then her eyes drooped in the trusting sleep of a newborn. Ellen had never experienced anything so precious, so fragile. This would only last a few moments.

Glancing at the observation windows, she became aware of an unfamiliar young couple. His navy business suit and tie complemented his six-foot height and blond crew cut. The lady appeared to be his petite counterpart with long dark curly hair framing a light olive Spanish complexion. Both watched Ellen and the baby with intense interest. Each appeared somewhat nervous and excited. Could this be Marie's adoptive parents? No! No, this was too soon!

Ellen didn't have long to wait. The hospital social worker walked in with a mask and gown. She approached the uniformed nurse and sleeping infant. "Since Baby Westin is sleeping, would you like to take her to her adoptive parents who are waiting outside?"

Ellen's heart plummeted. Yes, this was the moment she had promised for Rena's sake. And no, this was the last thing she wanted to do!

"I'll follow you," she said.

The social worker led her straight to the waiting couple. To insure the anonymity of the adoptive parents, no introductions were exchanged other than, "This is the nurse that assisted with your child's delivery," and "These are baby Marie Ellen's adoptive parents."

The adoptive mother's eyes glimmered with tears. Ellen held back her own tears, and as she relinquished the sleeping infant into the adoptive mother's arms, she blessed them with, "I will be praying for you as you care for baby Marie Ellen. Is there anything you would like to say to the biological mother who loves her very much?"

The adoptive father embraced the new mother and child. His face was wet with the unabashed tears of a full heart. "Yes, please thank her for entrusting us with the precious gift of Marie Ellen. We will do our best to care for her and love her."

The social worker led the couple and sleeping infant down the hospital corridor.

Ellen stood transfixed in the hall until they disappeared around the corner. "Goodbye, baby Marie Ellen. May God go with you." How could a piece of her heart have disappeared with such a tiny bundle? She could understand a portion of Rena's deep soul pain.

CHAPTER NINETEEN

Two weeks crawled along without a word from Eastern Mennonite College. Spring painted murals into the landscape with its tulips and daffodils and a glorious array of azaleas. The magnolia outside Ellen's bedroom window surreptitiously let go of its fuzzy winter flower buds. The huge, fragrant petal segments unfolded into striking pure-white blossoms. She marveled at the floral ballet swaying with grace in the breeze against the glossy forest green leaves of the magnificent forty-foot tree.

Mother Yoder always said, "When the magnolia tree's sweet fragrance fills the air, you know you're in Mississippi."

Ellen wondered, *Will I be here next spring or will I be in Virginia? And Lord, could you give me some clue as to what lies ahead? If not, help me put this whole college venture to rest.*

Out of consideration for proper protocol, she contacted Brother Matthew Troyer at mission headquarters to apprise him of Mr. Landamann's proposal and the need to apply to E. M. C. with promptness. Brother Troyer acknowledged her services thus far. He was pleased to hear of her willingness to further her education which would enhance her ability to serve in the future.

Pastor Don was reticent in his response to her leaving. "Ellen, you've been an integral part of the Missula Chapel team. I understand Mr. Landamann's perspective in needing to have a nurse prepared to replace Ms. Jacobs. However, you have come to love and understand our people who love you in return. Are you sure you want to leave now?"

He couldn't reveal he had subconsciously pictured Ellen becoming a long-term member of Missula Chapel. His eldest son, Lamar would be returning from a three-year PAX assignment in the Congo in eight months. He chided himself. *Why did I ever allow myself to envision Lamar and Ellen as a couple?*

Every day, Ellen watched for a notice in the mail. She had just returned from Winn Dixie with groceries when she picked up the ringing phone. A deep masculine voice said, "This is Robert Showalter, Dean of Students at Eastern Mennonite College. May I please speak to Ellen Yoder?"

"This is Ellen." Her breath caught in her throat. Would this conversation end with an *I'm sorry but. . .*?

The Dean continued. "I have your application in front of me for the 1966-'67 academic year. I am impressed with the in-depth statements of your academic and spiritual goals. Your transcripts verify that you meet our scholastic requirements."

Ellen breathed a bit easier. Would this be another turnaround, a rotation of the axis of her life like the call had been from Brother Troyer from Mission Headquarters?

"Our main ladies' residence, North Lawn, is full for the coming school year."

Her heart sank to her shoes.

"However, we are committed to making it possible for RNs to obtain their B. S. N. and we are expanding the program. We are especially interested in RNs such as yourself who have either been, or plan to be, in missions. Thus the top floor of the Administration building has been designated as housing for our more mature female students."

Listening to Dean Showalter's judicious choice of words, Ellen swallowed a giggle. He didn't use the term "older." At age twenty-two, she didn't feel like some "mature" matron.

"Does this interest you, Ellen?"

"Yes. Yes, it interests me very much. But I must be honest. Without financial assistance, I won't be able to attend. Would there be any financial aid available?"

"We've anticipated your question. In conjunction with our financial aid officer, I have put together a financial assistance package that would carry you through the two-and-one-half-year B.S.N. program. It combines scholarships, work-study options and a partial student loan. In the interest of time, we've already mailed this package to you. Please read it carefully and return it at your earliest convenience."

He wouldn't need to ask her twice.

"Feel free to call me with any questions." Dean Showalter concluded, "Your registration will be considered complete once we have your signature on the financial aid application. Have a good day."

"Th—Thank you, Dean Showalter," Ellen stuttered, rarely at a loss for words. "I'll give it my prompt attention and be back in touch." Hanging up the phone, her knees felt like an ice cube on an August sidewalk. Looking up toward heaven, she cried, "Lord I asked you for some kind of confirmation and you've sent me a roadmap for the next two years. Thank ya, Jesus!" She did a very un-Mennonite jig around the room.

Anne Maria and Ellen breezed into the nurses' residence, stopping to check their mailboxes. The financial and orientation packet arrived only two days after the Dean's phone call.

"Anne Maria, look at this!" Ellen scanned the contents of the bulging brown envelope, reading bits and pieces. "I am pleased to inform you that you have been accepted as a full-time student at Eastern Mennonite College for the 1966-'67 academic year. In light of your previous courses at a major university, you will be classified as a junior student. . . Please note the enclosed financial aid offer. . . which should cover your financial needs for the B. S. N. program. . .." Ellen let out a whoop!

Anne Maria laughed. Joining her friend's exuberance, she waltzed Ellen into the residence Victorian living-room. "I am so happy for you. Now sit down and tell me; when do you need to leave Missula?"

"Hmm, I don't know. Let me check. It says; in addition to an ample scholarship from the Mennonite Women's Service Commission, and a modest student loan, we are offering you a work-study position at the reception desk of the North Lawn ladies' dorm. It will include operating the telephone switchboard.

"Isn't that delightful? I would have been willing to scrub toilets."

"You didn't answer my question. When do you need to leave?"

Ellen perused the information packet. "They require all student work-study personnel to arrive on campus two weeks prior to the first day of fall classes. I'll be given one week of orientation and then I'll be asked to welcome and orient incoming freshmen. This means I need to be there by mid-August."

"Mid-August? Sister, that gives you two and one-half months. Is that enough time?"

"It will need to be enough time." Then reality set in. "Anne Maria, I'm going to miss you so much. I wish you were going with me," Ellen enfolded her dorm mate in a quick hug.

"And I will miss you too, my friend. But I am perfectly happy as a licensed practical nurse right here at Missula General."

Both fell silent for a moment.

"What if I make a mess of orienting those freshmen, or what if I have a hard time learning to operate the switchboard?" Fear of the unknown began to erode Ellen's self-confidence.

Chuckling, Anne Maria folded her arms and shook her head at the absurd suggestion of Ellen being inept. "When it comes to orienting those freshmen and conquering the switchboard job, I would say that if you can supervise Missula General, you'll most certainly have the skills needed to meet the requirements of your work-study assignment."

Ellen's crooked smile lent credence to the nonsense of her own fears. "Thanks, Anne Maria. You're the world's best encourager.

Besides, my father reminds me the Lord will step into my tomorrows before I even get there."

Ellen called for an appointment with Mr. Landamann. Walking into the executive suite felt very different from her previous appointment with the hospital CEO. The prospect of returning to academia left a fluttery, empty feeling in her stomach.

With God's help, what was there to fear? She sat up straight and alert. Anticipation banished her nervousness.

Bypassing his secretary, Mr. Landamann's towering figure beckoned from the inner door. "Ms. Yoder, welcome. Do come in and have a seat. Can you give me an update regarding my proposal in our last meeting?"

"I can, sir. This morning I received confirmation from Eastern Mennonite College in Harrisonburg, Virginia that I have been accepted as a fulltime student for the 1966-'67 academic year. They are offering scholarships and a financial aid package which would make it possible for me to attend.

Mr. Landamann, when you first suggested that I apply for my B.S.N., I wasn't certain that I wanted or needed such an academic degree. Today, I'm excited about the proposed venture."

"How do your parents feel about your leaving Missula General and the church community?" Mr. Landamann knew the local Mennonite community was very cautious about endorsing any form of higher education.

"My parents helped me sort out the pros and cons of staying in Missula versus returning to college. They support my decision even though they cannot contribute financially. They've made it a practice of encouraging each of us adult children to follow God's Spirit, whatever he speaks to our hearts."

Mr. Landamann nodded. "Wise parents. I highly respect the wisdom and faith of Mr. Dan and Ms. Francis. How soon do you need to leave Missula General?"

Having anticipated the need for a termination date, Ellen handed her letter of resignation to Mr. Landamann. "I need to be on campus by mid-August."

He nodded."That gives me a bit over two months to find your replacement. I shall get in touch with Mr. Troyer today. Perhaps he will be able to send us another Mennonite nurse to fill your current position. Thank you very much for giving us advance notice."

"Mr. Landamann, I have one more concern. I'm still not certain that I'll be able to develop the skills to do well as a Director of Nurses in this setting."

"Ms. Ellen," he said, using her first name for the first time. "I have seen many nurses enter and exit through this portico." The hospital CEO turned his leather chair to gaze through his office bay window, which gave him a full view of the ornate front entrance leading into the rotunda. A laconic smile lit his patrician face. "Some nurses have had leadership potential and some have not."

He turned back to Ellen. "How about allowing me to be the judge of your skills? Within the next two or three years, you may even become more comfortable with the possibility. We will miss you and so will the folks out at Missula Chapel. In the meantime, I'm recommending you pursue a B.S.N. Once you walk across that stage with a diploma in hand, y'all come back to see me. Ya, hea?" Smiling warmly, Mr. Landamann unfolded his lanky frame to shake her hand.

"I hea," she replied in the local vernacular. Smiling, she extended her hand. "Thank you, sir, for the invitation to return to Missula General. You have been very gracious. I'll do my best as a student."

"I'm sure you will. Have a good day, Ms. Ellen."

Ellen walked back to the nurses' residence with a spring in her steps. Just thinking about enrolling in a college where she knew no one generated a mixture of apprehension and excitement. Two weeks ago I was convinced it was too late to enter college this fall. God must be swinging open some improbable doors and I will embrace the challenge.

CHAPTER TWENTY

*M*om Yoder and Ellen plunged headlong into the college-prep mode. Ellen would need more than nursing uniforms for a collegiate campus. Like during her high school years, the two went "shopping" for clothes by visiting department stores to observe current trends. Then they would go home to recreate something similar to what they had just observed. Unless an outfit or item was drastically reduced, they rarely purchased it.

Exiting Belk's department store, Ellen spotted a pair of red, one-inch heels with a decorative strap over the instep and fashionable pointed toes. She tried them on. "Mom, look at these. They are size four and one-half and are a perfect fit. Besides they're on sale for only two dollars. Sometimes having small feet is a definite asset." Ellen placed her hands on her hips. Her eyes sparkled. "Hmm, I think I shall purchase them."

Mom smiled. If she thought they were a bit too fashionable for a Mennonite young lady, she refrained from throwing ice on Ellen's enthusiasm. She knew her daughter's tastes included a hint of pizzazz. No wonder her high school classmates had affectionately dubbed her "Sparkie."

"We have one more stop to make. If we hurry, we'll have time to visit the Missula Fabric Shop," Mom urged.

"I'll be right with you," Ellen said as she purchased the shoes.

Within minutes they entered the fabric shop. "Now the real fun can begin. This feels like Christmas in June," she exclaimed to her mother. The fabric store contained aisles of fabrics, patterns, buttons, trims and zippers. In hushed, excited tones, she whispered, "Wow! Where do we begin?"

"Just visualize what you admired in the department stores. Then pick a pattern that is most like those outfits. That will give you the direction you need to choose the color, type of fabric and accessories that you need."

"Thanks Mom. What would I do without your seamstress advice?" Ellen squeezed her mother's arm.

Her mother's smile lit her whole face.

Hours later they exited the shop, laden with shopping bags of materials they would need to create a college wardrobe.

During the next two weeks on her days off work Ellen cut fabric according to the selected patterns. As Mom fed the fabric between the presser foot and the teeth, the sewing machine hummed a steady song. If Ellen preferred a variation of a given pattern, her mother deftly made the adjustment while still protecting her daughter's modesty. Anything too suggestive or too tight or too short was abandoned. Three days of teamwork resulted in five new outfits that rivaled anything they had seen in fashionable dress departments.

Day one, her wardrobe had expanded to include a pleated pink-grey plaid skirt and pink blouse accompanied by a black cardigan plus an emerald green jumper to be worn with a beige blouse featuring a classic bow at the neckline. Day two produced a rust–brown tweed a-line skirt and dark brown jacket highlighting Ellen's dark brown hair. By five p.m. they had also completed a red and white mini-print shirtwaist with a matching red fabric belt. Filmy scarves would serve as accessories since jewelry was not permitted.

Ellen glanced in the full-length mirror on the third day of their sewing marathon. She was trying to stand perfectly still for the last fitting of the last dress. "Oh, Mom, this is my favorite!"

Mom chuckled. She was marking the hemline with seamstress chalk. "I think you've said that with each outfit."

"But that was before I tried on this one. This navy-blue dress sporting a white sailor collar and a circle skirt is so—just right. My red shoes will be the perfect accessory, which matches the narrow red trim on the collar. Thanks, Mom, for all your hard work."

"You're welcome." Mrs. Yoder stood to her full four-foot, ten-inch height. A beaming smile creased her face, all for the satisfaction of a job well done. Now her youngest daughter could return to campus knowing her wardrobe would not be elaborate, but feeling confident it would be adequate when paired with what she already owned.

Time was evaporating. In order to purchase a plane ticket, Ellen would need to sell her treasured VW bug. The 1960 silver beetle with its invigorating sunroof had become a part of her identity. Besides, the stick-shift vehicle was fun to drive and gave her a great deal of independence.

"Ellen, don't become so independent that you don't need a husband," Her father cautioned, and she rolled her eyes at him. He meant well and was concerned for her, but she had other goals in mind right then.

She stepped into the Missula Clarion office to place an ad in the weekly newspaper. "May I he'p you, ms?" the man asked, emerging from behind an enormous desk in the smoke-shrouded room.

"Yes, sir. I would like to place an ad in the Clarion to sell my car."

"Used cars are a dime a dozen. But leave your ad and I'll see it gets published. The printing fee is five dollars. You'll see the ad in Friday's paper."

"Thank you, sir. I shall look for it." Ellen considered the five-dollar fee exorbitant for such a short ad. She didn't waste any time paying the money and exited the office, wondering if it was worth the effort.

Wednesday morning brought a phone inquiry. "Ms. Yoder, this is Ted Boykin from the Clarion. I was setting up your ad for Friday's publication. It looks like a car I just might be interested in. Could I come out and take a look at it?"

She paused. "Yes you may, Mr. Boykin. It'll be available this afternoon at the nurses' residence after five p. m." Ellen's father had volunteered to assist her in the sale of the car so she wanted to give him time to complete a day of work.

Her dad stopped by the nurses' residence on his way home from work. Mr. Ted Boykin and his brother appeared promptly at five o'clock. "Hello Ms. Yoder and Mr. Dan. Had I known I was dealing with Mr. Dan's daughter, I would have given you cash for the car before you walked out of the office."

Ellen felt privileged to be known as her father's daughter. "Thank you sir, for your confidence in us but I'm sure you will want to take a test drive with my father." Ellen stepped aside. The two gentlemen, accompanied by her father, took the car for a spin on the highway.

Within twenty minutes the men returned. "That's a fine little car you have Ms. What is your asking price?"

"I need nine-hundred dollars, Sir."

Mr. Boykin rubbed his chin. "Ms. Yoder, nine-hundred dollars seems pretty pricy to me for a five-year-old car."

"Mr. Boykin," her father said. "You know us well enough that we wouldn't ask a dime more than the car is worth. It has low mileage and runs economically. Besides, my daughter has worked as a registered nurse at Missula General for minimum wages in order to serve this community. Now, at the request of Mr. Landamann, she's headed back to college to obtain a Bachelor of Science in Nursing. Your nine-hundred dollars would be a big help in that direction."

"If that's the case, let me congratulate you, Ms. Yoder on your endeavors. See'in as how I do like the way that car handles and it sure does have a pretty silver shine, let me give you that nine-hundred." Mr. Boykin proceeded to dole out nine, one-hundred dollar bills.

She smothered a gasp. She had never seen that much cash in one place at one time. She had purchased the car with monthly payments. Ellen had the definite impression the man would have paid more if the asking price had been higher but she wanted to be fair to the buyer. As she handed over the keys, a huge lump formed in her throat. Mr. Boykin drove away with her treasured little Beetle.

Pop slipped his arm across her shoulders and drew her close. "The Lord gave and the Lord has taken away; blessed be the name of the Lord."

Ellen exhaled slowly. "Yes, blessed be the name of the Lord. I asked God for a buyer and He sent one before the ad was even published. He provided the money I need for my flight plus funds for textbooks. Thanks, Pop, for helping me with the sale. Strange how selling a VW bug can clip a gal's wings."

"You'll fly again, *glennie* Betsy."

She smiled at his use of the German word for *little*. He'd always see her as his little girl. Their shared laughter dispelled her gloom.

Ellen's departure was only a week away. She both anticipated and dreaded her last Sunday at Missula Chapel. This would be the most difficult of her goodbyes, but she also had a ray of hope to share with Shonia. In the past months, she'd had few opportunities to spend time with Shonia except for brief informal chats after church. Several weeks ago, Brother Don prepared the close-knit congregation for her exit by announcing her future college plans and departure date. Shonia watched her with sad, questioning eyes wherever she went.

This morning Ellen joined the group of women carrying food to the kitchen for the monthly fellowship meal which would follow today's worship service. A festive feeling was shared among the group, though Ellen couldn't quite identify it.

Stepping into the church foyer, she was greeted by Shonia. "Come sit with us." Shonia led her to the Tatum clan pew. Chief Tatum and his wife had come from Pine Ridge. Ellen assumed they had come to spend the day with Will and Shonia.

Ellen was delighted to see Anne Maria and Dixon. Working different shifts left little time for extensive interaction. Once Barry returned from the second bus run, the complete young adult mission team would be in attendance. A rarity, indeed.

While awaiting the bus's arrival, Ellen was eager to share her news with Shonia. "Shonia, this week I received a letter from the Bureau of Indian Affairs stating they would be offering free English classes in Louisville. The classes will be held two evenings per week to accommodate persons needing to work during the day. Are you interested?" Ellen had worked tirelessly to get approval from the State.

The sun came out on Shonia's face. "I learn good English? Yes, I go."

Then reality set in. "How can I go? Have no car." The old apathetic sadness reappeared.

"Please forgive me, Shonia. I forgot to mention, the Bureau will provide transportation for anyone needing it." Ellen had been certain the classes would never succeed without free transportation. Convincing the Bureau hierarchy of that need had been another matter.

"Talk it over with Will and let me know after church."

With the arrival of the bus, Brother Don called the people to worship. Ellen watched Shonia's look of despair seep away as they began to sing.

Sunday school and the preaching service were much too short. Ellen wanted to extend this special morning, absorbing and relishing every minute. When would she get to hear Shonia's beautiful contralto again or Brother Don's passionate preaching? What had happened to her in the past year? Choctaws had become her people. The same people she had resisted serving had enriched her life so much that leaving would create a hollow vacuum.

The instant the final *Amen* was pronounced, her little nephew, Anthony, appeared at her elbow.

"Hey, Anthony. It's good to see you, buddy."

"Hey, Aunt Ellen. Come, I want to show you something." He took her hand and led her down the aisle.

As if on cue, the whole assembly followed Anthony and Ellen into the small fellowship room that once served as the mail room in a community post office. Fifty people crowded into the cramped space.

"Surprise!" reverberated around her. A beautiful masterpiece of a cake stood proudly on a table, with groupings of sugar flowers around script that read, *The Lord bless you, Ellen, and keep you.* She glanced over at Anne Maria and raised an eyebrow and her friend nodded, affirming that she'd made the cake. What a wonderful gift.

Chief Tatum stepped forward. "Ms. Ellen, we *ya gogay*—thank you—for what you have done for our people. You have cared for our sick and for our souls. Please receive from our hearts this gift." The Chief presented her an artistic rendering of Missula Chapel on a twelve-by eighteen-inch canvas. In the lower edge of the painting was the artist's signature, Shonia Tatum. Inscribed on the back were the names of each attendee, from Chief Tatum to the youngest infant.

It took a long moment for Ellen to regain her composure. "Thank you for allowing me to become one of you. We have walked together through hard times and through good times. I shall carry you in my heart to Virginia."

As the guest of honor, Ellen was ushered through the buffet line first. Folks stopped by her table to wish her well. Finally she and Shonia had a quiet moment.

"Ellen, Will says I go to English classes. I learn good English."

Ellen hugged her. "I'm sure you will, Shonia. Tomorrow I will submit your name and contact information to the Bureau. They should be in touch with you within a month."

Saying goodbye to her friend was the farewell Ellen had dreaded most. Today, both could look forward to their futures with hope and anticipation.

Chapter Twenty-One

he flight to Virginia produced every bit as much anxiety for Ellen than the flight to Indiana had. Boarding in the urban Columbus, Mississippi, terminal had been a cinch. Finding her way through the metro Atlanta hub became overwhelming. She couldn't decipher the flight screens. Courteous Delta airline personnel directed her to the correct gate. Minutes before the last boarding call, she stowed her overhead bag, sank into her window seat, and buckled her seat belt.

From the air, the topography of Virginia was breathtaking in contrast to the lowlands of Mississippi. The majestic Blue Ridge Mountains wore a massive coat of forest green.

The regal Massanutten peak dominated the mountainous view. Ellen could almost hear snatches of a folk love song her father sang to Mother, "In the Shenandoah Valley of Virginia, lives a girl who is waiting just for me. . ." Was it possible she would find someone special too? She shelved the thought. She didn't come to Eastern Mennonite for that. Ellen was here to earn a Bachelor of Science in Nursing and she would pursue that goal.

Twelve hours after departure, Ellen stepped onto campus in the heart of the beautiful Shenandoah Valley. An imposing three-story administration building at the base of "The Hill," rose on the west side of campus. Ellen stood still, momentarily mesmerized by the wide, gentle slopes of the central lawn dotted with picturesque shrubs, flowers, and a sparkling fish pond amid curving walkways.

But she couldn't remain rooted to the bottom tier of three flights of steps leading to the registration office. She needn't worry about adding pounds in this setting, with many hills to climb.

Ellen had carefully selected her navy-blue sailor dress and red heels for travel. Knowing she was well dressed gave her confidence a boost. Her heart beat faster and her excitement grew as she faced this new chapter in her life.

Self-assured upperclassmen with badges breezed past her as she made her way to the front desk. A pleasant young woman with a soft Virginia accent asked, "May I help you?"

"Yes, I'm Ellen Yoder from Missula, Mississippi."

"Welcome to the valley, Ellen. I believe you'll be serving as one of the mentors for our incoming freshmen."

Ellen nodded.

"Here's your mentor badge which we ask you wear throughout the next two weeks. I will page our matron, Miss Derstine, who will guide you to your dorm room."

Within minutes, a gracious middle-aged lady entered the office. Her appearance typified the conservative Mennonite element of the Valley. Miss Derstine's nylon net prayer covering was nestled on top of her wavy gray hair which swept back into a neat bun at the nape of her neck. Her tailored white blouse and long pleated, turquoise blue skirt conveyed a modest, but not austere, lifestyle.

Miss Derstine's smiling eyes nabbed Ellen's attention. "Welcome, Ellen, to Eastern Mennonite College. We hope you'll like it here." Her warm handshake affirmed her gracious demeanor. "Come. Follow me and I will take you to your dorm room."

The energetic Miss Derstine picked up a piece of Ellen's luggage and proceeded toward the stairs. Wielding a large suitcase plus an overnight bag and purse made the ascent up two more flights of stairs no small feat for Ellen. They entered a long hallway lined with dorm rooms, then passed a large communal restroom and showers.

"Here is your room, my dear. The décor is sparse, but the view is spectacular."

Ellen caught her breath while taking in the scene before her. From her third-floor vantage point the afternoon sun played hop scotch on the mountain with shifting hues of blues and violets and greens from the valley floor to the pinnacle of the range. Every morning she would now awaken to a view of the blue-tinged Massanutten peak and the surrounding valley. How had she been so fortunate?

"You're right. The view is magnificent." Ellen's heart was filled with awe.

Reluctantly, she turned from the window. "Thank you, Miss Derstine, for giving me the opportunity to live in this room."

"As for the décor, it keeps pace with the past four years that I've spent in nurses' residences. I'm sure I and a roommate can soften it a bit."

"Your roommate is Nancy Weaver, a young woman from Pennsylvania who is also pursuing a B.S.N. She will be arriving in two weeks. Dinner is served at five p. m. in the dining hall located in the lower level of North Lawn. Your first mentor's orientation session begins promptly at six." After a few more instructions regarding schedule and mealtimes, Miss Derstine left.

Ellen turned in a slow circle, surveying her immediate environment. Miss Derstine had called it sparse. Ellen labeled it *severe*. The two windows were dressed in roller curtains and non-descript valances. The rectangular room with worn, wooden flooring had generous closet space—a plus for female students.

Two single beds, two narrow wooden desks, and two straight-backed chairs completed the furnishings. Ellen quickly unpacked her limited, but carefully chosen wardrobe, which she could mix and match for greater variety.

She had just enough time to slip into a fresh outfit before finding her way to the dining hall. A group of twenty badge-wearing students had congregated, waiting for the dining hall doors to open.

An outgoing blonde wearing a prayer covering greeted Ellen. "Hello, I'm Elizabeth Kauffman, but you can call me Beth." Beth continued by introducing a tall, lanky young man hovering nearby. "And this is my cousin, Roger Hartman. We're both from Millersburg, Indiana."

"I'm pleased to meet you. I'm Ellen Yoder, most recently from Missula, Mississippi. However, I graduated from Bethany Christian High School in Goshen, Indiana, before attending Parkview-Methodist School of Nursing in Fort Wayne."

The cousins chuckled. "Beth and I are also alumni from Bethany Christian," Roger said. How about joining us for dinner?"

"I'd be happy to join you. Thanks for the invitation."

Tales of high school episodes provided an immediate point of reference for the three Hoosiers. Their conversation was off and running during the dinner hour.

"I'm not sure I'll be able to answer all the freshmen questions," Ellen said, "since this is my first year on the EMC campus."

Roger grinned. "I'm beginning my fifth year here as a first-year seminarian with a double major in psychology and Bible. Feel free to check in with me. If I don't know the answer, I'll point you to a staff person who can answer them."

Beth, a junior in social work, was also rooming in the administration building across the hall from Ellen. "You'll catch on quickly. And none of us know the answers to every question."

Following dinner, the three friends strolled to the North Lawn conference room in time for the six-p.m. mentor orientation, which consisted of a campus tour, followed by an hour-long review of campus rules and guidelines.

Ellen was at ease with the stipulation that no slacks be worn by women on campus. She felt comfortable maintaining the male-female distinction.

She wasn't so sure about the expectation that a prayer covering be worn by female Mennonite students at all times. She understood a prayer covering signified adherence to the Biblical teaching of I Corinthians 11:5 and verse 11 that says, "A woman dishonors her head if she prays or prophesies without a covering on her head. . . . And judge for yourselves. Is it right for a woman to pray to God in public with her head uncovered?"

Many Protestant denominations interpreted the Corinthian passage as relevant only in early Church culture. Mennonites, especially eastern Mennonites, tended to take a more literal view. Ellen grew up wearing a covering for public and family worship. Now she would need to adjust to wearing it throughout the day, especially since Chapel would be a daily occurrence, and some professors began most class periods with prayer. While it felt a bit awkward, Ellen was sure she could make the adjustment.

Freshmen girls were as varied as a bag of mixed jelly beans. Ellen introduced herself to Jennifer Nafzinger from California and to her parents, Dr. & Mrs. Nafzinger. "Hello, I'm Ellen Yoder. Welcome to Eastern Mennonite. If you'll follow me, I'll take you to Jennifer's new home for the next nine months."

En-route to Jennifer's room, Ellen engaged her in conversation. "Tell me. What prompted you to choose a college located on the east coast?"

"Oh," volunteered the bubbly teen, "my parents are both E.M.C. alums. But of even greater importance is that my parents are moving to Pennsylvania which means they'll be only five hours away."

Dr. Nafzinger winked and smiled at his daughter. "We hope Jen will be as happy here as we were. Her mother and I met in Dr. Hostetler's biology class." He reached out and gently hugged his wife who looked at him as though he was still the best catch on campus.

"Here are the keys to your room, Jennifer," Ellen said as she offered the key. "Your roommate will be Velda Long who plans to arrive within the hour. And here's my contact information should either you or your parents have any questions. It's been a delight meeting each of you."

The next student burst into tears as Ellen guided her down the hall of North Lawn to the young girl's dorm room. Ellen assured the student and her parents she would be nearby to lend any support that was needed in the coming weeks. "I'll be serving as your Resident Advisor and try to answer each of your questions or find someone who can help us find the answer," Ellen promised.

By the end of the day, Ellen was worn out and hoped her duties wouldn't be so taxing on her.

Ellen didn't feel as confident as she appeared. Near the end of the first week, she noticed Roger had a way of emerging out of nowhere at frequent intervals. Whenever she encountered a knotty problem or issue, Roger knew what to do, where to go, or who to see. Was he being magnanimous or did his interest extend beyond being the answer man?

Thursday evening of the second week, Ellen was called to the third-floor hall phone.

"Hello, this is Ellen."

"Ellen, it's Roger. You've worked hard all week. You deserve a break. A group of us, including Beth, are going across town to James Madison University on Friday evening to see the stage performance of *The Sound of Music*. Would you like to join us as my guest?"

"That sounds like fun." Ellen didn't know how she felt about being Roger's guest. But she was eager to relax and to get off campus. Going with a group that included Beth, appeared safe enough.

Friday evening, she donned her favorite outfit, the navy sailor dress with red accessories.

The effect evidently wasn't lost on Roger. "You look like you're ready for *The Sound of Music*."

She flashed a smile. "I am."

He gave her a debonair bow then escorted her to the car where he opened the door for her.

The backseat was already occupied by a congenial threesome—Beth, her roommate Sara, and Roger's friend Paul. With a bounce in his steps Roger circled the car and they were off.

The play was a dramatic adaptation of the Von Trapp family's flight from Austria during the Nazi take-over. It precipitated a lively discussion among the students while driving back to the EMC campus. Their predominant question centered around whether it was ethical for one of the characters to lie in order to save the lives of the Von Trapps or if he should have turned them over to the Nazis.

Some asserted there was never an occasion to lie while others argued that one could avoid telling the whole truth in the face of life and death or the possibility of being deported to a Nazi concentration camp. The carload did agree that life doesn't always hold easy answers.

Walking Ellen to her dorm entrance, Roger said, "Ellen, I've enjoyed this evening with you. There's a Southern Gospel sing at Elkton Mennonite next Sunday evening. I'd like to take you if that interests you."

"That sounds interesting Roger, but I do have a prior commitment. Perhaps another time."

"Okay. I'll be in touch. Good night Ellen."

"Goodnight, Roger." Ellen slipped inside, relieved that he hadn't pressed her for the details of her prior commitment. All resident advisors in the women's dorms were planning a welcoming party for incoming female students. She might have been able to opt out. But Ellen wasn't convinced she was ready for another relationship even though more than a year had passed since she said goodbye to John. Could she trust another man or would she learn to care and then need to walk away for some reason? Ellen wasn't eager to revisit the pain.

CHAPTER TWENTY-TWO

N ancy Weaver arrived right on time. Ellen greeted her with warmth. "Welcome Nancy. I've looked forward to your coming. Please make yourself comfortable."

"Hello. I think we'll get along."

Ellen wasn't sure what Nancy meant by her cryptic response but concluded her roommate had a good heart and meant no harm.

Nancy appeared noticeably uncomfortable meeting strangers. She carried herself with a stiff marching gait as though she had grown up with a drill Sergeant. Her hair was parted in the middle and pulled straight back into a bun. An ample prayer veil covered her hair.

Ellen hoped they could become close friends in spite of apparent external differences and contrasting personalities. But within those first weeks she struggled to find common ground with Nancy.

Ellen and Beth walked to chapel together.

"So, how's it going with your roommate?" asked Beth.

"You've probably noticed, we don't have a whole lot in common."

Beth laughed. "That's an understatement, my friend. You mean you emerged from two opposite prototypes." She sobered. "How is that affecting you?"

Ellen shifted her books to her other arm and kept walking toward the chapel. She didn't want to disparage her roommate. "Well, her tastes and mine just happen to be different. For instance, when I suggested we soften the appearance of our room by purchasing light-colored Victorian tiered curtains, she nixed it with, 'That would look silly. I like our room just like it is.'

Ellen squared her shoulders. "I've decided to make the best of the situation." She glanced at Beth with a crooked, mischievous grin. "I did cheat a bit. To soften our sterile environment, I created a silk floral wreath for our door that intertwines our names."

"I noticed the welcoming touch and figured you must have designed it." Beth stopped to survey the "K" section of the auditorium. "I'd better get to my seat before the monitor takes role." She waved. "See you later."

Ellen waved back as she eased her way into the "Y" section.

Nancy preferred solitude while Ellen thrived on interacting with others. Throughout the initial week of classes, they were inundated with an avalanche of assignments, term papers, and projects. Nancy chose to study during every waking moment.

Ellen tried to follow suit, only to become anxious and frustrated. Sleep became difficult. She determined she would simply be herself. Using her datebook, she scheduled each of her assignments ahead of their due dates, leaving room for error and times of daily relaxation.

The semester rolled along. Nancy became a permanent fixture in her desk chair. She looked up as Ellen came in from an invigorating walk with Beth. "Where have you been? Don't you need to study?"

"I do need to study. Now that I've had a refreshing walk, this Probability and Statistics assignment will make more sense to me."

If Ellen spent time with Roger or other friends, Nancy's typical observation was, "I don't see how you ever get your work done. You spend so much time socializing."

To avoid disturbing her roommate, Ellen began studying in the library. It became clear to her, they were oil and water. Their expectations of a college roommate did not mesh.

CHAPTER TWENTY-THREE

*E*llen was scheduled to work the North Lawn switchboard. It was part of her work-study program which she enjoyed most. During a lull in calls, she dialed the Dean of Women's office.

"Hello. Miss Derstine speaking." The Dean's calm voice was the balm Ellen needed.

"Miss Derstine, this is Ellen Yoder. I will be finishing my shift at the switchboard in thirty minutes. Would you have an opening in your schedule for a brief appointment?"

"Certainly. My secretary is out for the day, so just knock at my door when you finish working."

Shortly after Ellen's shift, she gave a hesitant knock on the Dean's door.

Miss Derstine drew Ellen into her office and closed the door. "What can I do for you?"

Ellen exhaled. "I'm not sure if you can help."

"Try me." The Dean had a way of setting Ellen at ease.

"I feel like a total failure. Thus far, whenever two incoming students had a difficult time adjusting to each other, I've been able to help them hear each other and establish rapport. I haven't been able to bridge the gap between Nancy and me. Believe me, I've tried."

"I believe you. Tell me about it."

The Dean listened as Ellen described her attempts at establishing meaningful communication with Nancy. "There are days when I feel like I'm walking on egg shells. I've switched to studying in the library so I won't disturb her. I'm having a hard time sleeping because I can't relax in my own dorm room. I'm afraid my grades will slip." Tears spilled down her cheeks.

Miss Derstine squeezed Ellen's hand and handed her a tissue. "Ellen, I think it's time to make a change. You've tried and it's not working. Not everyone is compatible with everyone else. Your personalities and expectations of college life are very different from Nancy's. Not wrong, just different."

"What are you suggesting?"

"Would you be open to considering another roommate?"

"Yes . . ." Ellen's voiced trailed off, fearful of who Miss Derstine might have in mind.

"I can understand your caution. But I'm thinking of another resident advisor who lost her roommate last week due to the illness of her roommate's family member. Have you met Alise Hampton from Oregon?"

"Alise?" Ellen felt like a huge burden had just lifted. "Alise and I are in the same English Lit class, plus we've worked together well in the nursing lab. If she's open to the idea, I would be so grateful."

"Let me do a bit of exploring and I will be back in touch tomorrow."

Ellen left Miss Derstine's office, a ray of hope lodged in her heart.

Checking her mailbox after Chapel the next morning, Ellen found a note in a sealed envelope. The handwriting on the front was in Miss Derstine's familiar, beautiful script. Ellen held her breath as she tore open the envelope.

> *Alise says she would be happy to share a room with you. Stop by Room 121 on the first floor of North Lawn to make arrangements for the move*
>
> *Miss Derstine*
> *Dean of Women.*

Ellen let out a slow deep sigh of relief which felt like she'd been holding for most of the semester. "Thank ya, Jesus."

Stopping by Room 121 was a delight. Alise welcomed her with a hug and asked, "How soon can you come? Tonight?"

"I think I should talk to Nancy tonight. Tomorrow afternoon we have nursing lab from three to four o'clock. After lab, might be a good time to transfer my belongings, if that works for you."

"That's wonderful! I'll be there to help you move."

Ellen wanted to avoid hurting Nancy. They walked to the dining hall in tandem, but dinner was a silent affair. Nancy hated trivial conversations and Ellen couldn't think of anything intelligent to say in the immediate emotional environment.

Back in their dorm room, Ellen's back prickled in discomfort. The time had come.

"Nancy, I've wanted to talk about our relationship for some time."

Nancy looked nonplussed. "What do you mean? Talking about our relationship? I think its fine."

"What were your expectations of a college roommate, Nancy?

"Expectations? I don't think I had a lot of expectations since I've never roomed with another person. In nursing school, I had a private room."

"Oh, that helps me understand why you assumed my study habits would match your study preferences. I'm sure you've noticed our differences."

"I can't see how you ever get your assignments in on time. You're always socializing."

Ellen nodded. "People do energize me and you need solitude in order for you to do your best work. Your method of studying is valid and works for you. It doesn't work for me. That doesn't make your preferences wrong and mine right. We're just different."

Her hands were clammy and she could feel her leg muscles tighten. "In light of the differences in our personalities, I have requested a transfer in dorm rooms." She feared Nancy's anger most.

Nancy swallowed, nodding in agreement. "That might make things better for both of us. When were you thinking of moving?"

"Miss Derstine sent me a note today, notifying me of an opening in North Lawn." Ellen bit her lower lip to keep from smiling. "I plan to move tomorrow afternoon after lab."

"Is there anything I can do to help you?" Nancy asked. "My assignments can wait for an hour tonight."

Ellen managed to keep her jaw from dropping. "Thanks so much for your offer. I would be happy for your assistance in getting my luggage and several boxes from the storage room. I'll try not to be too disruptive as I pack this evening."

Alise appeared the next afternoon with a friend in tow to help Ellen with her move. The gals accomplished the move in short order.

In the weeks that followed, Ellen could be herself again, making occasional interactions with Nancy much more enjoyable. If Nancy and Ellen had been oil and water, Alise and Ellen became peanut butter and jelly.

Roger kept appearing in the library, sometimes asking Ellen to join him for lunch or going for a walk up the Hill or for a date. He loved to sing and arrange music. Ellen was a clear soprano, so harmonizing was a delight while driving down Mount Clinton Pike or in a church service. Singing duets added spark to the relationship.

A letter arrived from Ellen's friend, Rachel. She and Dale were planning to come to Harrisonburg for Homecoming. Roger knew both of them and had always admired their vocal abilities.

Roger suggested he and Ellen combine their voices with the Stutzmans to sing as a quartette at a Youth for Christ musical rally.

The Stutzmans were enthusiastic about singing with Roger and Ellen. It was a fun evening, especially when the audience requested the quartette do an encore.

Throughout the weekend Rachel observed Roger's relationship with Ellen. The minute the two young women had some one-on-one time, Rachel probed, "So how do you feel about the man?"

Ellen laughed. "How am I supposed to feel?"

"That's not my question. 'Fess up, my friend."

"I'm glad you asked. I've been trying to interpret what I'm feeling and thinking. We have a lot of fun together. Plus, we share common interests, particularly music . . ." Her voice trailed off. Ellen's forehead wrinkled.

"But. . .?"

"But there are times when I get uncomfortable. Remember Roger's a Psych and Bible major. It seems everything I do or don't do, gets psychoanalyzed. It makes me weary." Ellen's shoulders slumped.

"You don't sound overly excited."

"I guess I'm not. For instance, if I raise one eyebrow, I'm challenging him. If I lift both eyebrows, I'm surprised or shocked. When I walk with both hands in my pockets, I'm attempting to hide my thoughts. And woe-is-me if I wear my red shoes because I must be feeling flamboyant."

"The relationship doesn't sound exactly heart-warming," Rachel said.

Ellen shrugged. "I've had enough psychology to know fifty-five percent of what we communicate is non-verbal. While non-verbals don't lie, they can be misunderstood."

"And sometimes you feel misunderstood."

"Precisely. Most of the time I simply attribute his observations to the fact Roger is getting his feet wet in the field of psychology. I make a convenient client." Ellen's smile was pensive.

"Something else bothers you."

Ellen shook her head. "Rach, you should have been the psych major.

You're right again. When Roger and I are together, we have lots of theological discussions. As a seminarian, he has classes in Biblical higher criticism. I don't think it's wrong to examine your faith in light of God's Word. But he seems to doubt the basic premise of salvation.

I tell myself we're just good friends. Yet neither of us is dating casually as though we were sixteen-year-olds. I'm beginning to question whether I'd want him to be the spiritual leader of our home, should this relationship progress any further."

Ellen gazed out over the Valley. "If I'm honest, I'm still looking for a young man whom I can trust to share my faith, my love, my hope for a family and my life-goal of serving God and the Church." She tilted her head to one side and pursed her lips. "Maybe that's just a pipe-dream."

"No, it's not an unrealistic dream. Be aware God may have someone else in mind to occupy that place in your heart."

Rachel hugged her friend then checked her watch. "Dale is waiting for me, so I must go. You can rest assured God will show you what direction to go. Remember, in order for a relationship to grow, it must be built on the bedrock of trust. Love cannot coexist with distrust."

The Massanutten exchanged its cloak of green for a dazzling wardrobe of yellows and reds and oranges. The Valley stood on the threshold of winter. At the Thanksgiving banquet, Roger was his old chivalrous self with no psychoanalytical comments. Ellen had an enchanting evening and relaxed, basking in his recurrent affirmations.

Later in the student lounge, Roger turned to her, "Ellen, I enjoy being with you. Is it okay if I keep calling you?"

Ellen hesitated a few seconds. "I enjoy being with you too, Roger." *Most of the time.* She didn't dare verbalize that thought.

"I do have one request. Since we have term papers to write, projects to complete, and finals to study for, I suggest we limit our dates to no more than one in a two-week period until the semester ends. Does that sound acceptable to you?" Ellen had been feeling the pressure of sustaining her honor roll grades in order to maintain her scholarships.

"It's not what I would choose, Ellen, but I'll honor your request," Roger said. "Here's a photo of myself for you. I hope it will make you just a wee bit lonely. I'll see you soon." Without asking, Roger kissed her lightly on the cheek and strode out the door.

Touching her face where he planted the kiss, Ellen felt a combination of surprise and chagrin. Had she been right in putting more space between their togetherness? When she kissed John goodbye, she vowed she would never kiss another man unless she was engaged to him. *Roger, I like you a lot but please don't trespass that boundary.*

Ellen's journal: January 10, 1967

> *I was in the library studying for a final in Genetics. Roger stopped by and asked to walk me back to the dorm. We broke-up tonight, but it doesn't really*

seem like a break-up. It's more like a parting of two friends. I had a feeling it was coming. Perhaps he went away more confused than I am. We decided not to date.

It's strange. I prayed a great deal about our relationship because I wasn't sure we should continue dating. Coming up to my room tonight, I didn't feel like crying or like my world has crashed. I feel more at peace than I have for weeks.

For some time, I've been wondering where this would lead us. Some of his faith issues could be a significant barrier in our marriage. I asked myself, "Do I want him to be the father of my children?"

He encouraged me to date others. I told him it would be more difficult for me to date again, but I would think about it. He said I'm everything a young man could ask for in a girl. I don't think he's in love with me, and

I'm not in love with him. However, his sensitivity helped me feel special.

In parting, he told me the story of "The Heart of a Beautiful Rose." There was a large rose garden. They had all been touched except the most beautiful one in the center of the garden. Roger said he wanted to touch the beautiful one, but felt he had no right to do so, lest he mar or damage it in some way. What did he mean by the story of the rose?

If Roger sees me as the rose, perhaps he is correct that I have been holding myself aloof, waiting for the right gardener.

CHAPTER TWENTY-FOUR

$\mathcal{E}$ldon Beachey glanced around the EMC library. Living in off-campus housing had its disadvantages. He couldn't retreat to a dorm room if things got too distracting in the library. Carrying a double major of Psychology and Bible gave him the advantage of camping out in the quiet Seminary corner booths. Today he needed quiet.

The more he tried to study for finals, the more Eldon agonized over the letter he had written to Rosalie. He remembered the moment they met at Levering Hospital in Hannibal, Missouri. He was an orderly and she a student nurse. Her gorgeous blonde hair first caught his attention. Her kindness and gentle spirit with patients kept his attention.

Eldon had been an active member of the young adult group at Hannibal Mennonite. Rosalie became a part of the group even though she was of a different faith. Her church adhered to some doctrine that was in direct opposition to Anabaptist Mennonite tenets. Rosalie kept saying she was going to become a Mennonite. She just never got around to doing it.

Eldon was vaguely bothered by the discrepancy between what she said she would do and what she was doing. They had dated on a casual basis, or so he thought.

As he was leaving for college, Rosalie asked, "Eldon, could we stay in touch by writing while you are away at college?"

"That sounds like a good idea. Keep me posted on what's happening in Hannibal."

Campus was a lonely environment for Eldon until he began to connect with other students by becoming a part of the outreach team at Gospel Hill Mennonite. Rosalie's chatty letters of Hannibal brightened his endless days of study.

It was soon apparent that what he thought was an innocuous gesture on his part of agreeing to write, Rosalie interpreted as a serious romantic interest. A week before Christmas break, she announced via letter that she had purchased a one-way bus ticket to northern Indiana to meet his family and to spend Christmas with him. She was asking him to make the seven-hour road trip to take her home at the close of the vacation.

Her letter threw Eldon into turmoil. What was he going to do now? What would he tell his parents? His sister's wedding was scheduled for December twenty-seventh, and he was to be their best man. He'd never thought of Rosalie as more than a great friend—one he liked and respected. She obviously thought of him as her boyfriend. Although he was not ready to commit to marriage, he decided it was high time to think of Rosalie as his girlfriend. He only hoped his sister would understand him bringing someone to the wedding.

He called home. "Mom, I've told you about my friend Rosalie from Hannibal. Is it alright if she comes to our house for Christmas break? She would like to meet our family. Is this a bad time because of Sara's wedding?" Eldon didn't mention that Rosalie had already purchased a one-way ticket.

"Oh. That would be nice. Your father and I would like to meet her. And you know your sister. If Rosalie is your friend, Sara will be her friend as well. But I'll check with her and call you right back."

Without hesitation, Sara welcomed Rosalie's proposed visit. She even adapted her plans to include Rosalie as one of the wedding reception servers. Eldon let out a huge breath. He could count on his family to come though.

In spite of differences in Christmas traditions, Eldon and his family enjoyed Rosalie's visit. She grew up with a Christmas tree. Eldon did not. Although she grew up in the city, she seemed to be acclimating to the more casual farm setting.

Late one afternoon, Dad Beachey asked Eldon to get a load of firewood with the tractor and trailer. After a semester of studies, Eldon relished the invigorating snow-covered outdoors. Wanting to share the experience with his new girlfriend, he asked, "Rosalie, would you like to go with me on the tractor to get a load of firewood?"

"I'd be happy to go with you." Rosalie had a way of emphasizing the term *you*, quickening Eldon's heart rate.

They donned heavy coats, headgear, gloves and boots and headed out to the tractor and trailer.

"Rosalie, all you need to do is stand here on the tractor drawbar. Put one hand on each fender and ride along." Eldon thought it a simple procedure. His sister had done it countless times.

Rosalie looked askance at the drawbar but shrugged her shoulders and said, "If you say it's safe, I'll do it." Climbing up, she clung to the fender. Eldon drove very carefully so as not to frighten her.

Task completed, the two made their way back to the farmhouse to wash up before supper. Without warning Rosalie exploded. "That was a crazy thing you asked me to do! I could have fallen off and been crushed under the wheels of that monster. What do you think I am, some farm girl?"

"I'm so sorry, Rosalie. I simply wanted to share what I thought was a fun job. I won't ask you to do that again." Eldon was completely baffled at her outburst.

Rosalie's anger subsided as quickly as it had erupted. For Eldon, the episode raised a flashing red light.

What had he gotten himself into? Rosalie was a nice person, but she had an explosive quality as part of the package. Everyone has some weaknesses. She should be allowed a few, he reasoned.

But he'd had all the rejection he wanted from his stepmother. Mom had a hard time accepting him and his biological siblings. She's been very kind in accepting Rosalie. Yet he never knew when her rebuffs would surface.

There must be some accepting, loving women in the world. His biological mother, Naomi, who died when he was only four-years old, was that kind of woman. While she lived his world was a safe, comfortable place. How would life have been different if she had lived?

Those questions haunted Eldon a thousand times during his formative years. Now the questions resurfaced in his relationship with Rosalie. If only he could find someone like Naomi. He wasn't ready to settle for a life of conflict and the pain of rejection.

The return trip to Hannibal highlighted other differences. When he turned the radio to southern gospel music, she switched it to country or rock. His family had welcomed Rosalie, but when she and Eldon entered her home, her brothers and father were in the midst of a card game and scarcely acknowledged his presence.

It was comforting to be able to say he had a girlfriend. And she did like him enough to pursue him boldly. That was a switch from Mennonite girls who were subtle in their approach to men of interest. Her visit raised questions of faith and a plethora of doubts regarding their compatibility.

Back on campus Eldon turned his attention to studies, and he continued writing to Rosalie. Writing was not as comfortable as it had been before Christmas. Whenever uncertainty appeared, he looked around, observing lots of dating couples. He reassured himself that he too had a girlfriend. Yet he had this nagging fear he was walking into a turbulent relationship, which was getting in the way of concentrating on his studies.

Eldon prayed about his situation. He knew it was possible to be comfortable in a distant, non-committed relationship, but a close marital relationship could be very painful for both of them.

Lord, I don't want to hurt Rosalie. We don't share the same spiritual or family values. She doesn't deserve to be hurt, but I don't want to lose her friendship. I'm not sure we could bond enough to make our marriage work. Please show me what to do.

He hadn't meant to lead her on or to hurt her. She really was a fine young woman. He wouldn't play games with her feelings. The longer he procrastinated, the more painful breaking up would be for both of them.

Concentrating on hermeneutics took a sheer matter of the will. In spite of his best efforts, his mind kept doing flip-flops. It would flip to the letter he had mailed. He knew how long it took a letter to travel from Virginia to Missouri and mentally tracked it all the way. Today was the third day. He kept picturing Rosalie opening his letter and knew she would be crying.

There must be a way to soften the pain. No matter how hard he tried, he couldn't shut out the sadness he was feeling for her. He choked up just thinking about it.

Eldon and another male student shared a room in a private home at the edge of the campus. He kept thinking about Rosalie's pain while walking to the Kreider residence.

Mrs. Kreider met him at the door. "Eldon, we received a call from a young lady wanting to speak to you. I told her you would be home this evening by nine o'clock."

Before he could escape to his room, the phone in the living room rang. "Eldon, it's a long-distance call for you." Mrs. Kreider smiled as she handed the phone to him.

If only he had a phone in his room, but there was only one phone in the house. He was sure Rosalie had received his letter. Sensing his need for privacy, Mr. and Mrs. Kreider retreated to the kitchen.

"Hello, Eldon speaking."

The voice on the other end of the line was familiar. "Hello. I got your letter today."

He could hear the tremor in her voice. "Did you meet another girl on campus?"

"No. But I've come to realize there are enough differences in our beliefs, likes, dislikes, in your past and mine, that a continuing relationship would be very difficult for both of us." He avoided mentioning marriage.

"I'm sure we could work out our differences."

"While we could work at them, I'm convinced it would not be the most satisfactory relationship for either of us."

"I would like to try. Can't we just continue to write and see if we can work on those issues?"

"I really don't think that's a good idea. The longer we continue this relationship, the harder it will be for both of us later."

"Are you sure there's not someone else?" Rosalie sounded skeptical.

"No there really is no one else. I have no one else in mind, and I've not dated anyone else since coming to E.M.C."

"Well, if there's no one else, then won't you reconsider?"

"No. I gave this careful thought before I made this decision. I wouldn't play games with your emotions by being undecided."

"Well then, this call is on my dime. I'll keep you on the line as long as I can." They talked a while longer clarifying whether or not they would return the Christmas gifts they had exchanged. Neither wanted a return of the gifts. Loneliness slithered across the phone lines. Both were in tears as they ended the call.

Oh God, what are you trying to teach me? I've just said "goodbye" to one of my best friends and it hurts. Please ease her hurt.

CHAPTER TWENTY-FIVE

*A*lise and Ellen pooled their efforts in studying for the Probability and Statistics final. Professor Sauder had assured the class that if they mastered the ungraded Prob and Stat pretest, they would do well on the final exam. Calculators were banned in the classroom, so understanding how to solve any given problem was of utmost importance.

One section of the pretest stumped both girls. Frustrated, Ellen said, "Alise, how about going with me to the library to see if any other students from our class are working on this? I'm getting nowhere."

"Certainly. Let's go."

Glancing around the crowded library, they spotted a group of three gals pouring over their Prob and Stat texts.

Ellen led the way. "I see you're working on Sauder's pretest too. May we join you?"

Dawn, who sat near Ellen in class, looked up. "Sure. Have a seat. Maybe you have the answers to problems ten through twelve."

Alise groaned. "Answers? No way. We've been slaving over that section for the past hour."

"Five heads should be better than two. Let's see if we can figure them out together," Ellen said. Thirty minutes later they were no closer to a solution then when they began.

Alise looked around the library. "So, who else is in here that's taking this course? Ellen, do you see that guy sitting in seminary corner? His name is Eldon Beachey. Why don't you go ask him if he's figured out this segment of the test? He's pretty good at math."

"Why should I be the one to check with him? I don't know him from Adam. At least you know his name. I've seen the guy in class, but I've never even said, 'Hey y'all.' Alise, why don't you ask him to help us with the equations?"

"Because you're a better math student than I am. Between you and Eldon, you just may be able to formulate the right answers. As you Mississippians say, "Ya hea'?"

Ellen had determined to make the switch to Yankee vernacular once she arrived on campus. Sometimes she forgot, much to the amusement of Alise.

"I hea'. See y'all at lunch." Before she could lose her resolve, Ellen made her way to seminary corner

"Hello Eldon?"

The studious young man looked up from a seminary text. "Hello. May I help you?"

His demeanor was considerate which gave Ellen the courage she needed. "I hope so. My name is Ellen Yoder. I believe we're in the same Prob and Stat class. A group of us have been trying to decipher the last section of the pretest without success. I thought I'd check to see if you might have been able to crack Sauder's code. Sorry to bother you. I see you're in the midst of hermeneutics. Would another time be better?"

As if on cue, the bell rang for Chapel. Eldon grinned. "I'm not getting much out of hermeneutics and should be switching to Math. How about checking back with me after Chapel?"

"That's kind of you. I'll be back." Ellen was anxious to find a way to master the Prof's pretest. She had a grade point average to maintain.

Eldon joined the wide stream of students finding their alphabetically assigned Chapel seats. A hush descended on the

assembly as the college president stepped to the podium. Eldon's mind was anything but hushed. He was still processing last night's phone call from Rosalie.

He frowned. Who was this Ellen Yoder? He vaguely recalled seeing her in class. One could scarcely be totally oblivious to the attractive petite brunette, but he'd tuned out all females on campus.

Within minutes of Chapel dismissal, Ellen made her way to Eldon's study corner. He ushered her into a seat. "Are you ready to tackle sections ten to twelve?"

When she smiled, the sun came out. "I'm ready if you are. I have a hunch, if we combine what you know with what I know, we may come up with the correct answers."

For the next hour they worked together, yielding one success after another. Eldon glanced at his watch. They weren't done and the cafeteria would soon be closing for lunch. He had a problem. What was he to do with this young woman he scarcely knew? He wasn't ready to invite her to accompany him to lunch. The pain of losing Rosalie's friendship was still too raw.

"We're going to miss lunch if we don't get to the cafeteria pretty soon. Let's break for lunch. We can meet back here at one o'clock to pick up where we left off."

Sensing his discomfort, Ellen slid out of the booth. "Sounds like a plan. Thanks so much for your help thus far. See you later." Ellen waved and walked toward the cafeteria.

Lest he convey the wrong message, Eldon made sure he delayed leaving the library until she was out of sight. He wasn't interested in pursuing a friendship at the moment.

Eldon found a spot in the slow-moving line toward the trays and food. After a bit, he heard lively chatter coming from a group of girls moving through the line four or five students ahead of him. He could see the group was clustered around the girl who had requested his help with math. She appeared to be a catalyst among her friends. Obviously, they respected her.

While working on math, he noticed Ellen had a keen mind. She was easy to work with. He hadn't thought about who she was or what kind of person she might be. *I wonder why others seem to be drawn to her?* He neared the end of the serving line.

Alise called to him. "Eldon, come join us for lunch?"

He wasn't excited about joining a bevy of girls but didn't see any of his buddies, and he had no reason to be rude to Alise.

"Lead the way, Alise, and I'll meet you at a table." At least he knew Alise's name and had just spent the past hour with Ellen.

When he got to the table, Alise made introductions. He learned Ellen was an RN who had returned to college from a mission assignment to earn her B.S.N. in Nursing.

By one o'clock, Eldon and Ellen were back at work. They conquered the rest of the Prob and Stat pretest with ease by coordinating their efforts. Ellen gathered her text and notebook. "Thanks so much, Eldon, for your help. I enjoyed working with you." She smiled that captivating smile he'd seen several times since they started studying together. "Now, I feel ready for tomorrow's exam."

"And thanks to you, Ellen. Combining our problem-solving skills cut down my cram time. You're a team player. I hope the exam goes well for both of us."

The exam did go well. Both aced the test.

Except for grieving the loss of Rosalie's friendship, Eldon assumed life would soon return to normal.

CHAPTER TWENTY-SIX

Phone calls from home were rare for Ellen. A long-distance pay call was reserved for emergencies or some exceptional news. Letters would need to suffice. Mother Yoder's letters kept Ellen in touch with Mississippi happenings.

Dear Ellen,

The burnings and bombings seem to have quieted for the moment. One never knows what will happen next. Shonia was able to enroll in an 'English as a Second Language' night class. Will's not ready to take the risk. Please pray for her safety.

I was relieved to hear you're no longer seeing Roger. I sensed he wasn't what you are looking for in a husband.

Love,

Mom

P.S. Pastor Don's son, Lamar, is due back in the States in two weeks. I don't believe you've met him. He's a lot like pastor Don. Missula Mennonite is looking forward to his return.

Ellen mulled over the note. She thought She'd hidden her inner questions regarding Roger and his seeming spiritual instability. Mom had a remarkable sixth sense. Was she hinting that Ellen might want to meet this young man whose life goal probably includes missions, specifically Missula Mennonite Mission?

Lord, I really don't know where you want me to serve after I get my degree.

Working at the switchboard in the main lobby of North Lawn gave Ellen a great deal of exposure as to who was dating whom. Young men came to the window asking to see their dates. Ellen's task was to page the young ladies. Observing the couples' delight in each other resurfaced Ellen's memories of dating John. There had been many concerts and picnics and walks and talks and . . . She needed to let go of the past and live in the present. Roger was a distraction, filling in the lonely spots of her heart. She liked him a lot but didn't learn to love or trust him like she did John.

Lord, I believe this is where you want me to be right now. Help me to be content and to trust you for my future.

Ellen hadn't noticed Eldon before their Prob and Stat cramming session. She never saw him with a girl on campus and assumed he was unattached. She was clueless that he had recently said goodbye to another girl.

Having only one class together didn't afford much opportunity to get to know this kind young man from Indiana. He was intelligent and seemed to value her academic bent. She found herself gravitating to the library to study.

Alise watched Ellen's subtle interest in Eldon. "So, you're going to the library to study," she teased. "Could it be that you prefer someone other than me as a study buddy?"

"Alise, you're a great study pal. But the library does increase the probability of interacting with . . ."

"With whom—a young man named Eldon who happens to be good at Statistics?"

"Hmm, you might be right, although I wouldn't admit it to anyone besides you."

Eldon couldn't ignore Ellen studying in the library a discreet two or three tables from his chosen spot. Had he been totally oblivious? Nah, he wasn't that preoccupied, but he had lost a great deal of study time vacillating over his relationship with Rosalie. At the moment, he needed to concentrate on his studies.

Was he imagining things or might there be some interest in a friendship? Occasionally they chatted. Then he chided himself. *I don't have time for a relationship. I have got to study. I can't afford to let my grades slip.*

In spite of his resolve, Eldon found himself watching Ellen to learn more about this intriguing young woman. He remembered a commitment he made to himself in fourth grade. He had been fooled into thinking a pretty girl his age was very nice. But when they played tetherball, she kept making mistakes. Instead of admitting her errors like the rest of the players, she repeatedly lied about them.

Eldon made a vow to himself. He would never let a girl know he was interested in her until he observed her for at least a month. He wanted to see what she was like "so she can't easily hide her real self from me." Eldon didn't want any nasty surprises and didn't want to be hurt again. He would watch quietly from a distance and see what he could learn.

The distance between them narrowed often. What began as casual chats progressed to more significant conversations. "When I was in first grade, my family lived in northern Indiana. I remember your family stopping by our house for a Sunday afternoon visit. I have no clue as to how our parents knew each other," Ellen said one day. At that point, their families lived twenty miles from each other and attended different churches.

"That's incredible. I honestly don't remember you. Please don't take that as an insult. I think I vaguely recall that day. Do you have a number of brothers?'

"I have seven brothers." Ellen chuckled. "You guys played softball all afternoon. When it came to softball, short kid sisters were considered a liability, not an asset."

Shortly thereafter, Ellen's family had moved to southern Michigan. Their paths didn't cross again until their teen years. Eldon learned she had been part of a northern Indiana touring choir. "If you sang in the Gospel Chorale, do you know my twin cousins, Ann and Jan?"

"Yes, I do. I was part of an octet that sang at Ann's wedding. We were asked to sing a cappella from the church balcony. That was a beautiful experience."

"Amazing. I was an usher at Ann's wedding and must have escorted your ensemble into the reserved section of the balcony. Sorry, I didn't notice you that day." He laughed.

She smiled, "And I didn't notice you either."

Learning that their lives had intersected before created an intangible sense of trust in this fledgling relationship. They discovered their families held similar values. However, when Eldon revealed he was carrying a double major of Psychology and Bible, Ellen became a little more reserved toward him. Cautious. It didn't make sense, but he wouldn't let that get in the way of their friendship. Yet something was drawing them together like donuts and coffee.

One Friday night, the switchboard calls had been brisk. A green light flashed with a call from Elmwood, the men's dorm. "Good evening, how may I direct your call?'

"Hello, Ellen?"

Ellen sat up straight, certain the deep masculine voice belonged to Eldon Beachey.

"Yes, this is she." She inhaled and held her breath.

"Ellen, this is Eldon Beachey. Two weeks from tonight at six thirty p. m., they will be showing slides of Russia in the Chapel. Would you consider going with me to see them?

He was asking her for a date? He had taken a while to make this call. In spite of his Psych and Bible majors, Ellen had decided that getting to know Eldon could be fascinating, but she would temper her response. "Hmm, that sounds interesting. I'd be happy to accompany you."

"After the slide presentation, we could stop off at the EMC and Messiah College basketball game if it's still in progress and if that interests you."

"I enjoy watching basketball, and the competition between EMC and Messiah should be a close one."

They decided on a time to meet.

Another green light blinked on the switchboard. "Eldon, I'll see you later. Another call is coming in so I need to run."

Ellen returned to work, but she wanted to dance.

Eldon hung up the phone from speaking to Ellen. His grin couldn't be contained no matter how hard he tried. Waiting a month and observing her was worth it. He needed to be sure. But there's this other girl, Emily, in his German class who sort of looks like his biological mother. What would it be like to date someone tall and soft spoken like Mother? On the other hand,

Ellen has Mother's gentle personality. Besides, she's a cute, petite brunette. He was interested in Emily but intrigued by Ellen. He'd need to check this out by process of elimination.

The end of Ellen's switchboard shift couldn't come fast enough. She had to tell Alise. She was on a swift walk to her room, then skidded to a stop.

The door to Emily Weaver's room was ajar. She wouldn't have dreamed of eves-dropping on someone else's conversation. Hearing Eldon's name caught her attention, though.

Emily was speaking. "You've got to hear this. This morning Eldon Beachey walked me from German class to the chapel. He asked me for a date! He's taking me to the Intercollegiate Quiz Bowl at James Madison University next Friday night." Her voice was laced with anticipation.

Ellen did a double take. He's taking Emily to the quiz bowl this coming week and me to the Russian lecture the following week? So, he's not interested in limiting his options. She didn't like that. Who did he think he was—some Romeo?

Then she remembered he's from Indiana. In that Mennonite community, there's a common practice to date casually until one is ready to make a commitment to "go steady." He's free to date others, which meant Ellen had the same option. She'd hang on to her heart.

Her pace quickened. She didn't want to be caught listening. In spite of her mini self- lecture, she couldn't contain her news. "Alise, you'll not believe what just happened."

"Try me."

"The switchboard was really busy tonight."

"Yes, but that's not what you were about to say. Don't keep me in suspense."

"Eldon Beachey called to ask if I would go with him to the Russian slide presentation in two weeks."

"Wow! You've been hoping for a date with him for weeks, haven't you?" Alise gave her roommate a quick hug.

"I have, but that's not the end of the story. Just now as I was walking down the hall, Emily Weaver's door was open. She was all excited because Eldon asked her to the quiz bowl next week."

"Oh. What do you think of that?"

With a thoughtful, half- smile, Ellen said, "It's too early to jump to any conclusions. Something tells me he's the kind of guy who proceeds with caution. Until he's certain, he'll check out each option." She did a nonchalant shrug. "At least I'm in the running. I'll enjoy getting to know him better. I have this philosophy that each young man I date adds something valuable to my life, and I pray that I will add something positive to his."

Eldon wasn't into casual dating. By age twenty-three he had created a list of character traits he was looking for in a wife. He was sure that dating Ellen would be a comfortable experience, judging from their library conversations. But he didn't want to have second thoughts should their friendship lead to marriage. Dating Emily at least once seemed like a reasonable way to avoid making a mistake. Perhaps, he might even prefer Emily. He'd never know unless he tried.

Eldon escorted Emily to the North Lawn foyer. "Goodnight, Emily. Thanks for going with me to the quiz bowl."

Blushing, Emily looked at the floor and whispered, "Goodnight, Eldon."

His gait slowed as he approached Elmwood. He couldn't keep himself from comparing the two young ladies. Emily is a pleasant young lady, but she's so shy it's difficult to maintain a conversation. I'll always admire her but she isn't right for me.

He took the steps to the second floor two at a time. Now he was looking forward to dating Ellen exclusively.

Ellen crossed off the days in her date book. Lest she infringe on Emily's time with Eldon, she avoided studying in the library until after the quiz bowl. Then her chats with Eldon picked up where they left off. He was just as friendly as he had been prior to his date with Emily.

Alise was still up when Ellen came in from her date. "Tell me about your evening. I'm dying to know what you think."

"Hmm, I think it was an absorbing evening. The slides regarding Russia were informative and EMC won the game."

"Cut the rhetoric."

"You asked what I think. Were you really asking how I feel?" Ellen's eyes twinkled with mischief.

"Okay, okay, whatever you call it. I really want to know was it good, bad, or indifferent?"

Ellen laughed. "Alise, it was both delightful and comfortable. Comfortable in that we could talk about anything. I didn't hear any psychoanalytical jargon. So far, so good. It was delightful in that he asked me to go with him to hear the Augsburg Choir in two weeks."

"Wow, that's a formal concert. Not bad, my friend, especially since the Augsburg Choir is one of the highlights of this year's Lecture–Music Series."

CHAPTER TWENTY-SEVEN

ressed in her finest black dress and heels, Ellen walked into the North Lawn lobby to meet her date.

"You look very nice this evening." Eldon's smile lit up his face.

He offered his arm as they descended the dorm steps. They strolled across campus to hear the Augsburg Choir.

Ellen felt honored to be seen on campus with Eldon. He was dressed in a black suit, white shirt with a narrow tie secured with a tie tack. It had been a long time since she felt so special. She hoped Emily wasn't watching from a dorm window. She wouldn't want her to feel left behind.

At the close of the concert, the British conductor turned to the audience and invited everyone to join in singing a cappella "How

Great Thou Art." Ellen marveled at Eldon's well-controlled deep bass voice. She had no previous clue as to his musical abilities.

"This has been a wonderful evening, Ellen. I sing in a men's quartette. Next Sunday evening we're scheduled to sing at a Negro hymn sing. Would you like to go with me?"

Ellen didn't hesitate. "I would enjoy that very much." She still wasn't positive she could completely trust him, but she was having a great time. Was he the soul-mate she had searched for so long?

Their dates became a weekly occurrence.

His chivalrous attitude toward her began to put a chink in Ellen's self-protective armor.

Ellen sent a letter to her parents, filling them in on her growing interest in a young man named Eldon Beachey. Her mother replied almost instantly. Opening the envelope, a train ticket fell out.

> Dear Ellen,
> Your last letter is of great interest to your father and me. Is Eldon the son of Lee Beachey? If so, his father was born in your Grandpa Miller's home in Michigan. In order to obtain better

medical care, the Beacheys traveled from Illinois to Michigan. They awaited the arrival of their firstborn in my parent's "doddy has" (grandparent house).

My older sister and I vied to wash out the baby's dirty diapers because Mrs. Beachey paid us the handsome sum of five cents for every five-gallon bucket of diapers we washed. In 1916, five cents was a significant bonus for us at ages ten and twelve.

If Eldon is who we think he is, he comes from a fine family. Check it out and let us know.

So that's how her parents came to know Eldon's parents. Interesting.

The letter continued. . .

Pastor Don's son, Lamar, has arrived from the Congo. Before you give your heart away, you'll want to meet him. He slipped back into the Missula setting like a hand in a glove. Currently, he is

working as a forest ranger. His
enthusiasm for the Lord is contagious.

Easter vacation will be here in a few
weeks. Your father purchased a train
ticket for you. We are counting the days
until we see you again.

Much love,

Mom

Studies became a challenge when there were more interesting things to pursue. But Ellen was determined to maintain her grades. She wouldn't allow herself the luxury of squandering the opportunity to work toward her goal of achieving a B.S.N. People in Mississippi like Mr. Landamann, her family, and others would be disappointed if she didn't succeed. Her return to Missula General as a Director of Nurses' still left her with conflicting emotions, especially since meeting Eldon. How much easier it would be if the Lord revealed His will for her life via a message in the clouds or some direct voice from heaven.

Eldon & Ellen were swapping hospital stories on their scenic drive up the Skyline Drive. Having worked as a hospital orderly before coming to college, he understood and enjoyed her world. That was so different from John, who avoided all things medical.

After checking with his father, Eldon learned Lee was indeed born in the Miller household.

Ellen savored the previous connection with her mother's family.

Near the top of the Skyline, they stopped at a grassy meadow and stepped out into a gossamer world. Mountains shrouded with wispy clouds swirled all the way down into the Shenandoah Valley. An early warming trend produced prime picnic weather.

"Come with me. Do you mind if I take your picture?" Eldon was an amateur photographer. He wanted to capture this special moment.

Ellen was wearing a white dress with bunches of tiny purple violets printed in minute bouquets. The deep purple sweater draped around her shoulders was a complementary accessory.

"That's fine if I can also take a picture of you."

Eldon requested Ellen sit on a big rock for the photo. The early spring wild violets seemed to migrate onto the print of her full shirted dress.

Ellen needed a bit of guidance in learning how to operate Eldon's camera but soon mastered the mechanics of the *Ansco Autoset*.

Eldon sat down on the small boulder beside her. "Ellen, Easter vacation is coming. I'd like to take you home to meet my parents in Indiana. Would you be interested in coming with me?"

"I'd be honored to meet your parents. But my dad has already purchased my train ticket. I haven't been home for seven months so they are counting the days until I come home. I'm sorry, Eldon." She could see that he was disappointed.

Ellen wanted to meet the Beacheys, yet she longed to see her family. Then too, her parents wanted her to meet Lamar Mast. Were they secretly hoping Lamar might be a key factor in helping Ellen return to Mississippi after graduation?

"When do you need to leave for Mississippi?"

"I am to leave Charlottesville at five p. m. on Thursday evening. I'll travel through the night and arrive at home approximately twenty-four hours later on Good Friday evening."

"Then let me take you to Charlottesville."

"You would take me all the way to Charlottesville? That would delay your leaving for Indiana."

He nodded. "I know. It would also buy me some uninterrupted time with my favorite person. I can wait to leave until Friday morning without a problem. Is it a deal?"

"It's a deal. Thanks for your gracious offer. I didn't expect such kindness." She blinked back the tears that were forming. Ellen hadn't experienced this kind of consideration from a young man before. Her previous qualms about dating a Psych major disappeared in an instant.

CHAPTER TWENTY-EIGHT

Τ he train bound for Birmingham and Meridian roared into the Charlottesville station. Neither Eldon nor Ellen wanted their magic moments to end. Eldon helped check her baggage and turned to give her a brief hug. "Have a good time with your family. I'll be here when you return."

"Thanks Eldon. I'll look forward to seeing you when I return. Our sharing time en-route has been so special. Give my greetings to your family." With that, she boarded.

The last "all aboard" resounded through the terminal as Ellen waved from the passenger car window.

Eldon stood rooted to the platform, waving goodbye until she became a speck in the distance. He had never felt such a mixture of joy and desolation. The drive to Charlottesville would carry him through the next two weeks of spring break. He prayed for God to show him the way he should go. After all, Ellen may be the girl he'd been looking for.

He wondered, should I have asked her to go steady before sending her home? Going steady was a mid-western arrangement which meant they would date each other exclusively. Without that agreement, it was understood both were free to date others.

Train wheels clicked a constant high-speed rhythm as the Amtrak train raced south. Ellen replayed their conversations from Harrisonburg to Charlottesville. They discovered they had grown up in similar Mennonite churches. Christian values and a personal relationship with Jesus Christ served as the inner fabric of their belief system.

Eldon had examined and questioned the tenets of the Mennonite Church while in Voluntary Service, yet he firmly believed them. His faith basis was not blown away by the wind of theological arguments like Roger's had been. She could count on Eldon being the spiritual leader in their home if their relationship progressed. If she were to marry a Yankee, what would become of her vision for her mission among the Choctaws?

The phone rang at Ellen's parent's house around eight p.m. on the day of her arrival.

Mom picked it up and said hello. She listened briefly then said, "Yes, you may." Smiling, Mom handed the phone to Ellen. "It's Lamar."

"Good evening, Lamar. This is Ellen."

"Ellen, I know we've never met, but I'd like to take you out for dinner tomorrow evening, so we can begin to get to know each other. Does that interest you?"

"Lamar, I'd be happy to accept your invitation. However, I want to be perfectly honest with you. For the past several months I've been dating a young man on campus. We're not going steady, but I do consider him a very good friend. Under those conditions you may want to retract your invitation."

"Ellen," he said without hesitation, "thanks for telling me about my competition. but I'll take my chances. I do want to get to know you. May I pick you up at six o'clock for dinner at Boykin's Restaurant?"

"I'll look forward to it." At the thought of meeting Lamar, her stomach fluttered, then churned. *What if I'm beginning to love Eldon?* She was having a hard time focusing enough to unpack her suitcase.

Chewing the inside of her lip, she looked around as if looking for answers. Was she being fair to Eldon? He hasn't declared himself as to whether we have a future together. Her heart told her they might. Was she running ahead of God's will for her life by dating Lamar? Or was it a redirection of God's plan for her life?

Walking toward the back door, Ellen called to her parents seated in the living room. "Mom and Pop, I need a breath of fresh air. I'm going for a walk. I'll be back soon."

"There's a pleasant breeze. Have a good walk," Mom called from the couch where she sat crocheting.

Stepping outside, Ellen inhaled the evening air. The sunset spangled the sky with layers of light and color. *Is this call from Lamar, God's way of turning my heart toward home? I don't even know where home is anymore. Is this where I belong? Where do I belong?* The tangled cobwebs of her thoughts became less burdensome as she walked.

Dressing for a dinner at Boykin's was not a problem. The atmosphere would be dressy casual. Spring was in full swing in Missula with a profusion of azaleas, daffodils and tulips. Ellen chose a pastel pink dotted Swiss shirt-waist, complementing her brunette wavy tresses and fair skin.

At the stroke of six p. m. the doorbell rang. In her bedroom, Ellen gathered her purse and sweater. Late evenings tended to be cool.

Her mother answered the front door. "Hello, Lamar. Welcome. Do come in. Ellen will be with you shortly."

"Thank you, Ma'am."

Her father laid his Grit newspaper aside and rose to meet their guest. "Good evening, young man."

Ellen entered the living room and encountered the twinkling eyes of Lamar. So, this was the son of Pastor Don? His dark hair, tanned skin, kakis, and deep blue izod shirt highlighted his electric-blue eyes. Lamar's engaging smile put her at ease.

"This is our daughter, Ellen," Pop said. "Now you take good care of our 'glenne' Betsy and have a good time this evening." Only Pop could call her little Betsy and make it sound like an endearment.

Lamar gazed at Ellen. "I'm pleased to finally meet you, Ellen."

Ellen's heart skipped when he reached out to shake her hand. "I'm pleased to meet you too, Lamar."

Then he turned back to her father and said, "Mr. Dan, you can count on it. I'll take very good care of Ellen. We won't be too late."

The pair made their way to the car and Lamar opened the car door for Ellen with finesse.

"Thank you," she said as she slid into the front seat. She looked forward to a fun evening, but at the back of her mind, she couldn't help wondering what Eldon was doing that night.

Boykin's dining room was dimly lit, the soft golden light reflecting off the pristine white dishes and crystal goblets. White table cloths, rose cloth napkins, and colorful, fresh spring flowers on every table completed the ambiance. Lamar requested a secluded spot. They talked like old friends despite having just met.

"Why haven't we met before?"

Ellen smiled. "I assume it's because you went to the Congo while I was in Nursing School."

"That makes sense. Both of us had three-year commitments. We PAX men weren't given furloughs by our mission boards, so I knew I would be gone for the duration."

"And I had the privilege of coming home only once a year. My scholarship didn't cover travel."

Lamar glanced around and observed they were out of earshot of other diners. He leaned forward. "Dad tells me y'all initiated integration at Missula General. That took a lot of courage, especially after being targeted by the KKK."

Ellen was grateful for the privacy their table afforded. She blushed. "Thanks for the compliment. I didn't feel very brave the night Rena came in. I wasn't setting out to be a civil rights worker. My chief concern was protecting Rena in a hostile environment. I was certain it would cost me my position." There was something about Lamar that made it safe to share her real feelings.

"Well, it began a radical change at Missula General," Lamar said. "They solved the integration problem by creating all private rooms."

"Hmm, given that Mr. Landaman was concerned about being run out of town or being lynched, he found a way to circumvent the issue." Ellen continued, "It's a definite step up from having a 'white hall' and a 'black hall.' Private rooms were probably not what the U. S, government had in mind."

"Speaking of Mr. Landaman, I understand he was hoping you would consider preparing for the nursing directorship. Are you planning to return?" Lamar asked.

"I'll be back this summer to pick up several courses at Mississippi State before entering my senior year at EMC. Beyond that, I don't know, Lamar. I want to be open to God's direction, whether it be foreign missions or stateside. So, I've not ruled out Mississippi. I admit it's scary to think about coming back and facing the antagonism of some of my coworkers again."

He nodded. "I can believe that. But think about it. Missula General needs someone like you." His warm, approving smile told Ellen he was looking forward to her return to Missula. He stopped short of saying, *I think I need someone like you. We could be a great mission team, either here or abroad.* She shook off her ruminations. She was practically going steady with Eldon.

Talk drifted to his work in the Congo. Ellen could see that serving oversees energized him. "Tell me. Where do you hope life will take you? Is God calling you to remain here in Mississippi or are you thinking about returning to the Congo?" If she were to return to Missula General, would Lamar be elsewhere?

Lamar fiddled with his fork. "That's a fair question. Like you, I'm not exactly certain of when and where God wants me to serve. In the Congo, I had the opportunity to interact with several missionary pilots who flew our team to remote areas in the rainforest that sits along the equator. Those guys did a fantastic job." Animation laced his reply.

"Tell me about your time in the interior."

"We couldn't have reached some of the indigenous people groups without those pilots who risked their lives for us. Since the Congolese secured their independence from Belgium in 1960, there's been a great deal of political instability. I'm not even sure I could get back into the country at the moment."

"So now what?"

"Being a forest ranger gives me a lot of time to think." Lamar's eyes glowed with anticipation. "I've been thinking. Moody Bible Institute has a B. S. program that combines solid Bible and theological training with missionary aviation. I'll need to work at least a year to rebuild my reserves for tuition. Then I plan to apply."

"Sounds like a fascinating and rewarding plan. I'm sure you'll do a great job." So, he wasn't returning to the Congo right away.

The waitress slipped the receipt beside Lamar's dessert plate and said. "Y'all just take your time."

Ellen had been oblivious to their surroundings and she realized most patrons had already vacated the dining area.

"Maybe we had better leave before they throw us out." Lamar chuckled.

He checked his watch. "We still have an hour of daylight. Would you like to see what the world looks like from the top of a fire tower on private land?"

"That would be fascinating. Let's go."

The Mississippi topography was breathtaking from the fire tower vantage point. A brief evening shower had washed the world. As the sun began to set, God was hanging it out to dry. Pinks and blues and lilacs painted the vast expanse of sky. The sea of green below and the pungent pine scent of the laundered forest thrilled Lamar, and he hoped Ellen would feel it too.

"Lamar, I had no clue this corner of the world was so magnificent. And the silence is so awesome, it's like being next door to—"

"—to heaven?"

"Yes, it's like we're standing on holy ground." Her face was alight with the sacred beauty of the moment.

Lamar hoped there would be many more such moments. He slipped his hand over Ellen's on the railing. She was experiencing what he often felt when he stepped into the "top of the world."

"Ellen, thanks for sharing my cathedral in the pines. I promised Mr. Dan that I would take good care of you. I guess I'd better get you back to the house before your parents begin to wonder if their pastor's son is trustworthy."

Nearing Ellen's home, Lamar said, "Ellen, tonight has been so special. On Sunday evening, a southern gospel group will be at church. May I have the privilege of taking you to the event?" In the dim light, he couldn't read her expression. Was he pushing her too fast?

"Lamar, I would be happy to go with you."

He could sense a smile in her reply, and his heart did a little flip-flop.

The Sunday morning service was everything Ellen had envisioned. Shonia gave her a hug the moment she entered the Chapel doors, exclaiming, "Ellen, you're home!"

"I'm here for two weeks. Then I must go back."

She slipped into the pew beside Shonia and her family. Hearing the quiet cadence of Choctaw conversations surrounding her was like waking up in familiar territory. Her glance swept the small congregation that had become her anchor.

Intermingled among the Millers and Masts and Weavers and Yoders sat Rennies and Tatums and Warrens and Tubbys and Wesleys, plus other clans. These were her people. Was this where

God wanted her, or was she only called to serve there for a season?

Shonia followed Brother Don's sermon with intense interest. Ellen detected she was reading her English Bible with increased ease. The final benediction had been spoken when Ellen touched Shonia's arm. "Tell me about your English classes."

"I'm reading. I can understand Brother Don. I like the Jesus stories." The process of becoming literate was transforming the formerly timid Shonia.

"Have you thought about becoming an English translator for Choctaws?"

"A transla—tor?" Shonia looked confused.

"Yes. A translator tells the Choctaw person what the English person is saying and then tells the English person what the Choctaw person is saying. We need translators in hospitals, schools, and in many other situations. It could be a welcome relief from choppin' cotton."

"People pay a trans-lator?"

"Some schools and hospitals pay the translator for their services."

Shonia's face lit up. "I'll think about it and speak to Will."

"Keep learning, Shonia. You are doing very well. I'm right proud of you."

This was a victory for Ellen. To see something she started become a life-changing event for one of these people thrilled her. Her heart was torn between returning here after graduation or going elsewhere. I pointed Shonia in the right direction. Now if only I knew the direction I should take.

Sunday evening, Lamar and Ellen entered the Chapel together. People gave them nods and approving smiles as the couple joined the assembly in listening to the gospel singers.

The evening sailed by much too fast.

As Lamar prepared to leave the Yoders, he said, "Ellen, I'll need to be out on tower duty all week and won't be able to see you. Getting to know you has been an incredible treat. Could we see each other once more before you go back to EMC?"

"What did you have in mind?"

"Next Sunday evening is a joint Mississippi–Alabama youth rally in Meridian. The whole program is usually a great evening. Would you like to go?".

"I would enjoy that." The drive to Meridian would take an hour and a half. A bit more time, she thought, to get to know this young man who lived, ate and dreamed missions.

During the trip to and from Meridian, the two never stopped talking. "Ellen, I'm going to need to say goodnight, but I hope it's not goodbye. I really don't want to lose you. Would you consider staying in touch by writing when you get back on campus?"

"Lamar, I don't want to play with your emotions. These two weeks have been filled to the brim with getting to know you, besides reconnecting with my Mississippi family and friends. You've become a dear friend. So is Eldon." She shook her head. "I'm not sure how I'm going to sort it all out. Do you want to write to me under those conditions?" She didn't have a clue what to do.

Gently, he tipped her face up until her eyes met his. "I promise I won't rush you, Ellen. I didn't set out to complicate your life. Writing once a week may help you sort out those feelings. I'll take my chances. And yes, I do want to write. When the time comes, God will show you and me the way. We can count on it."

There it was again. The way. Could she trust God to show her how to unscramble her feelings? What if she listened to the wrong clues?

Chapter Twenty-Nine

*T*wo weeks of spring break were an eternity for Eldon. The separation convinced him Ellen was the young lady he wanted to pursue. The closer he got to the Charlottesville train station, the faster his little Corvair negotiated the serpentine Blue Ridge Mountain curves. He smelled car breaks and slowed his pace to the posted speed limits. He would arrive in plenty of time. Southern trains didn't run ahead of schedule.

Leaning against the outer wall of the brick train station, he heard a faint whistle way off in the distance. The rumble of the approaching train could be heard somewhere near the city limits. He checked his watch. Ellen would be here within minutes.

Our reunion will be sweet.

Eldon walked to the edge of the platform. A friendly engineer tooted his horn at every city railroad crossing.

The silver bullet thundered into the station with a blast of the whistle and screeching wheels. Eldon tried to catch a glimpse of Ellen through the coach windows as the train skidded to a stop. He couldn't see her. How would he ever find her in the throng of arriving passengers? She only stood four-feet-ten and three-fourths inches tall.

He chuckled. She blithely informed him an inch and three-fourths helped her pass the nursing school entrance criteria that all students be at least four-foot-nine.

Descending from the steps of a coach five cars ahead, he caught sight of a short young lady. He took off on a run. It had to be Ellen. Slithering through the crowd Eldon could see her receiving her travel case from a gracious, white haired conductor. Someone's been watching out for her. *Thank you, Lord.*

She turned to survey the crowd. Their eyes met and locked. Her face broke into a wonderful welcoming smile.

He closed the distance between them. Inhaling, he caught the scent of her floral perfume. Everything within him wanted to kiss her sweet lips, but this wasn't the time nor the place. The crowd rushed past them.

His knees felt shaky. He looked down at her. "You're back," was all he could muster.

"I'm back," she sighed.

"Let's pick up the rest of your luggage and get out of this horde." Eldon guided Ellen to the baggage claim area to retrieve her blue suitcase.

Ellen shivered. Was it from the cold Virginia air or from fatigue? They followed the crowd into the parking lot. Eldon kept his arm around her shoulders, attempting to shield her from the brisk wind. He wanted to protect her from anything that might hurt or distress her. Opening the car door, he ushered her in out of the cold.

"It's great to see you, but you look tired."

"Spending the past twenty-four hours on a high-speed train or in layovers has been exhausting. But it's so good to be back."

She didn't say "with you." Eldon attributed her reserved demeanor to fatigue. A night of sleep would bring back her sparkle.

Ellen's dorm mate, Alise, wrapped her in a bear hug the minute she stepped into their room. "Welcome back. Tell me about your trip home."

The drive from Charlottesville served to stir the kettle of Ellen's mixed emotions. Even though she wasn't ready to discuss it with Eldon, her roommate was safe. Brushing aside her immediate need for sleep, she said, "Alise, I've got to tell you what happened."

"I can feel a good story coming. Let's get ready for bed before you begin."

Within minutes, the two sat cross-legged on their single beds, separated in the narrow dorm room by a mere four feet. "Alise, I wasn't prepared to be introduced to a new super guy the minute I walked into Mom and Pop's home."

"What's he like, and for goodness sake, what's his name?"

"His name is Lamar Mast who happens to be our pastor's son. He's a returned PAX man from the Belgium Congo."

"You haven't told me what he's like? What does he look like?"

Laughing, Ellen said, "Give me time and I'll get there. He's a southern gentleman who rarely forgets to treat you like a queen. He has a slight build and the bluest eyes you've ever seen."

"How tall is he?

"Tall? Hmm, I didn't think about that a whole lot. Seeing as how you're five-foot-ten, I guess a guy's height might be important. I'm not sure of his exact height. He's a bit shorter than Eldon."

"That makes him at least six inches taller than you are. Oh, to be petite."

"Oh, to be tall and willowy like you. I guess we'd both better be satisfied with the inches we've been given."

"I guess you're right, but one can dream."

Alise regrouped. "Back to the Congo. Is it coincidental that he's interested in foreign missions? You thought that's where God wanted you."

"I don't know if it's coincidental or if God wants me to reconsider. Two years ago, I was sure God was asking me to go into foreign missions," Ellen reflected, "but when the foreign door closed and a stateside setting opened, I realized God can use me wherever I happen to be on this planet."

"So now the question remains, do you accompany Eldon into his calling or Lamar into his God-given niche?" Alise had a way of sizing up the crux of any issue.

"The rest of the question is how and when do I tell Eldon about Lamar? Lamar knows about Eldon."

"Good question."

"The three of us are young adults. I get the distinct impression that neither Eldon nor Lamar is interested in dating casually like we might have when we were teenagers."

"And Eldon hasn't asked you to go steady."

"Exactly."

"So, if Eldon were to ask you to commit to a long-term relationship, what would you say?"

"I've asked myself that exact question over and over during the thousand-mile train ride. If he had asked me to go steady before the semester break, I would have said yes in a heartbeat. Since he didn't, I can't be sure of his intentions."

Ellen grew thoughtful. "Eldon is the kind of young man I've been looking for during the past five years. He's intelligent and kind and thoughtful and sensitive and encouraging and handsome to boot."

"I get the picture. So what's the problem?" Alise grinned and shook her head.

"The problem is, do I follow my heart or is God trying to redirect my attention? Foreign missions is where I'd be if my relationship with Lamar led to marriage. His goal is missionary aviation and I could learn to care for him.

"Eldon is a psych and Bible major which will probably result in a stateside ministry somewhere above the Mason Dixon line. Eldon and I share a common Yankee heritage. Lamar understands my adopted Mississippi world."

"Girl, it sounds like you need to totally rethink your future. This still leaves you with the complicated task of telling Eldon about Lamar."

Like breakers on a stormy beach, a wave of fatigue washed over Ellen. She cradled her head in her hands. "I know. I know. But first I've got to get some sleep."

CHAPTER THIRTY

*E*ldon couldn't help but notice that since Ellen's
return, her typical spark wasn't there. She remained
pensive and quiet for several days. Perhaps she'd
been ill.

"Are you feeling okay?" he finally asked her.

"I'm fine." She did a poor job of smiling.

"We do have a campus doctor, you know."

"I know. Don't worry about me."

Eldon let it pass. Something was bugging her. She'd put up an
invisible wall between them that he couldn't scale. Did this mean
the beginning of the end of their relationship? What had he done
to precipitate the distance? He cared a lot more about this
relationship than he thought he did.

Ellen was the first young lady he met that seemed to have the same warm, caring personality as his biological mother, Naomi. The loss of his mother left a deep, empty void in his heart. Would he lose Ellen too?

What if Ellen wanted to end their friendship and was trying to think of a gracious way to approach him. Had he deluded himself into thinking she was like Naomi? Was he attracted to her merely because of the similarity in their personalities? The "what ifs" taunted and tormented him.

Later that day, Eldon walked into Carl Keimer's room after quartette practice. He could count on his quartette buddy to shoot it straight.

"Carl, I haven't a clue what's happening with Ellen. Before spring break, things were going great between us. Now, I'm not sure what's going on."

"So, how's it different?" Carl leaned back in his desk chair and stretched his long legs out before him. Eldon had his full attention.

"Before the break, she was warm and accepting. We could laugh or share whatever weighed on our minds."

"I noticed. Seemed like the two of you were inseparable."

A wry smile tugged at Eldon's lips. "She wasn't eating breakfast until I convinced her that eating three meals a day was healthier than eating two. Being a nurse, she couldn't refute the logic."

"And you expanded your time together."

Eldon cocked his head. "You've got that right. But that was before the break. Now we're doing good getting together for two meals a day. Most of those are either eaten in silence or spent in surface chit chat." His forehead burrowed into a troubled frown as he thought a moment about Ellen's sudden back pedal. "Maybe our relationship wasn't as good as I thought. Maybe I wanted to believe we had begun to really care about each other."

"What are you going to do about it?"

"What do you mean? What am I going to do about it? I've thought about breaking up if the relationship isn't going to go anywhere."

"Before you throw in the towel, why don't you talk to her?"

Eldon felt nonplussed. "I have talked to her. I'm telling you, I'm not getting anywhere."

Carl shook his head. "No, no. I'm sure you tried to let her know you care about her. That's fine, but you're spinning your wheels, bud. Ask Ellen what happened."

"That seems pretty risky."

"Is it any riskier than ignoring the problem?"

"No. I'd rather know than live with the unknown. Thanks Carl." Eldon stood to leave. "Maybe, there's some hope."

Eldon and Ellen emerged from the dining hall into the Shenandoah twilight. The Virginia countryside awakened into an I'm-glad-to-be-alive kind of spring. Redbud and dogwood trees marched up the path on the Hill behind the Admin building. Campus was decked out in tulips, daffodils, and forsythia.

Eldon reached for Ellen's hand. "Would you like to climb the Hill?"

"Yes, let's get some fresh air."

Eldon thought he detected a renewed lilt in her voice.

They ascended the Hill in companionable silence, each drinking in the beauty around them. The path was a paved, meandering, narrow walkway. At the crest of the Hill, the sunset was painted in lavenders, pinks, and blues which had begun tucking behind the valley for the night.

No one occupied the stone bench positioned under the sheltering branches of a pear tree, decked out in pure white blossoms. They gravitated to the bench, gazing out over the valley.

Eldon broke their quiet reverie. "Ellen, I don't know what's different. Before spring break our relationship seemed free and open. What happened to change it? Did I do something to offend you?"

"No, you didn't do anything to offend me." Ellen looked up at Eldon.

"Then what's wrong? It feels like there is this invisible *something* between us. I need to know what's going on."

Ellen took a deep breath. "You're right. Things have changed. I wanted to tell you when you met me at the train station, but I was so confused I didn't know where to begin."

"Begin anywhere."

"Is it right to assume that we've come to care about each other as special friends but that we're not going steady?" Ellen searched his face.

"I'd say that's correct. So, if we care about each other, why can't we connect like we did before the break? Two weeks shouldn't make that big a difference . . ." his voice muffled into a bewildered silence.

"Eldon, there's no way I want to hurt you. If I've been more reserved this past week, it's because I was trying to figure out a way to tell you about my trip home."

"I'm listening."

"I'll try to begin at the beginning. If something doesn't make sense, you can stop me." She proceeded. "The night I arrived at home, the phone rang. It was our pastor's son, Lamar Mast."

"So, there's another guy?"

"I thought you said you were listening,"

"Sorry."

They both laughed. It cleared the air.

"You asked if there's another guy. The answer is yes and no. While I lived in Mississippi, Lamar was gone in PAX Service which you know is the Mennonite equivalent of the Peace Corp. He returned in January of this year. Apparently, his family told him about me. When he discovered I was returning for spring break, he promptly gave me a call."

"He didn't let any grass grow under his feet," Eldon quipped.

"Are you listening?"

Their laughter diffused the tension.

"So . . ."

"So, I told him about you. I informed him I had been dating a young man on campus for the past three months. We had become great friends, but we weren't going steady. Under those circumstances, I gave him the option of retracting his invitation. Instead, he reiterated he at least wanted to get to know me."

Eldon leaned a bit closer, his shoulder touching hers. "Smart guy."

"Long story short—we had three dates. Before I left, Lamar asked to write once a week until I return for the summer. I reminded him I would probably be dating you back on campus and that he might want to reconsider his request. He decided to take his chances."

"Thanks for telling me about Lamar. It's a huge relief to know I didn't do something that caused the distance between you and me. Did I ever tell you, you're not a very good actress? One thing I admire about you is your honesty. At least now I know what, or rather who, is my competition."

"Eldon, I really do value our relationship, and I want us to get to know each other better. Can we do that until we know what direction our future might take us?"

"What about Lamar?"

"I appreciate and respect both of you. I'd like a bit of time to sort out my feelings. Does that seem fair?"

Conflicting bits of resistance and relief flitted across Eldon's mind. "I'd like to say no, it's not fair. I don't want to share you with anyone. On the other hand, I want you to have the freedom to choose. A forced or premature decision wouldn't help any of us. As long as you're open with me and with Lamar, I can live with it."

"Wow! Just hearing you say that makes you even more special." Ellen exhaled a deep sigh of relief as though she had been holding her breath for days.

Eldon didn't like that he had competition, but he'd do what he had to do to give himself a fighting chance with Ellen. He hoped he'd win.

Chapter Thirty-One

*I*f Probability and Statistics ignited Eldon and Ellen's relationship, musical events began to shape and mold it. Each sang in the oratorio, *David the Shepherd Boy,* plus participated in area Gospel Sings. Ellen sang first soprano in a lady's sextet while Eldon sang bass in a male quartet.

The weekly letters from Lamar kept Ellen in touch with Mississippi while communicating his longing to see her. "I'm counting the days until you return to attend summer school at Mississippi State."

Ellen tried to make answering his letters a priority. Sometimes it was difficult when studies and spending time with Eldon occupied most of her time.

Eldon invited her to attend the spring banquet—the college's finale for the year. A week before the banquet, a note from the campus postmistress appeared in Ellen's mailbox. *Please pick up a package from Mississippi.* This was the first package she had received since arriving on campus.

Alise caught up with Ellen as they scurried to their room. "It's my mother's handwriting," Ellen noted. "Finances are tight for my parents so I can't imagine what she would be sending."

Ellen opened the tissue-lined box. A tiny gift card decorated in violets lay on top of the tissue. She picked it up and read it aloud. "The card says, *Happy Birthday, Ellen, a week early. Love, Mom. P. S. I thought you might need a special dress for the banquet.*" She pulled open the tissue and both girls gasped.

"I can't believe it." Tears formed in the corners of her eyes as Ellen gingerly picked up one of her mother's dress creations. She stroked the delicate white, whipped-cream fabric. "This is incredible." The full gathered skirt had an exquisite embroidered overlay skirt made of white nylon, topped in the center of the waistline with a fabric bow. She wondered what sacrifices her mother had made in order to send the gift.

"That is gorgeous!" Alise exclaimed.

Alise ran next door to borrow a full-length mirror, propping it against the wall. "There. You've got to try it on. Now!"

Ellen didn't need a second invitation. Slipping the dress over her shoulders, she turned to let Alise zip up the back. The bodice was a perfect fit. The dress had a rounded neckline and elbow-length sleeves—a flawless top for the street-length skirt. Simple, modest, and so feminine.

"You are going to wow that young man. Rick and I are going to be in the lobby when Eldon comes to pick you up. I have got to see his face when he lays eyes on you."

With a self-conscious giggle, Ellen slid out of the dress. She hung it cautiously in her closet. She would steam out a few wrinkles before 'The Night.'

Banquet night arrived. Alise and Ellen spent several hours preparing and primping. Every hair had to be in place. They helped each other fashion a stylish French twist. Each topped their dark-haired updo's with a round, five-inch, nylon-net prayer covering. Wearing a prayer covering symbolized their willingness to acknowledge the headship of God and man. Most female Mennonite students wore them.

Ellen stepped into her white heels, complementing the white dress.

"Do I look okay?"

"Okay?" Alise laughed. "Dear, you look more than okay. You look absolutely lovely!"

Alise needed the same reassurance. "Do I look acceptable?" Stately Alise was in a mint green, A-line taffeta dress and beige dress flats.

"Alise, Rick will be right proud to escort his elegant-looking date to the banquet." On occasion, Ellen's Mississippian vernacular still surfaced.

Butterflies circled in Ellen's stomach. She checked her watch. Rick had called for Alise five minutes ago. Just then the hall intercom announced, "Ellen Yoder, please come to the lobby. Your escort is in the lounge area."

Eldon, stood waiting, erect in a black suit, white shirt, narrow black tie complete with tie tack, corsage in hand—the first corsage he'd ever purchased. Nothing but the best would do for Ellen. He ordered it to fit her personality. He hoped she would like it.

Finally, the door opened and Ellen stepped out. He caught his breath. The only word he could think of was *stunning*. But he wouldn't feel comfortable using that word. Mennonites didn't use superlatives unless you knew a person really well.

She glowed as she came toward him. He met her, hands outstretched, his heart alight with love and admiration. He drew her into the nearby alcove. If only he could kiss her.

Bending down, he whispered, "You are so beautiful." *Keep your cool. Kissing her would be premature.* Besides, college protocol called for restraint in open displays of affection in public areas.

She smiled up at him. "Thanks for the compliment, Eldon."

Presenting her with the corsage, he said, "This is my gift to you."

Ellen's eyes grew wide with awe. "Oh, how lovely!" Nestled in green floral grass, lay a medium-sized corsage of five diminutive, red sweetheart roses tied with embossed white ribbon. As Ellen attached the corsage to her dress, a camera flashed. Looking up they caught Alise laughing and slipping a camera into her purse.

Alise and Rick waved as they exited the lobby.

The decorated banquet hall lent an enchanted atmosphere to the evening. Spring flowers surrounded a splashing water fountain. Candles flickered in the subdued lighting on every table. The couple made their way to a table where Rick and Alise sat. Ellen's whole body tingled when Eldon gave her shoulder a gentle squeeze as he seated her, then took his seat beside her. She caught her breath. *Is he feeling what I'm feeling?*

She looked out over the banquet hall. Hundreds of other couples in formal attire lined pristine tables bedecked with rose petals. Crystal goblets filled with sparking grape juice awaited them. Rick and Eldon were dorm buddies, so conversation and laughter flowed easily throughout the gourmet ham dinner served on pure white china.

A stringed ensemble with harp accompaniment played softly in the background. The elegant dessert of red velvet cake and ice cream were served when Eldon caught the glimmer of candlelight reflected in Ellen's dark eyes.

For one long cherished moment, it was just the two of them.

A quiet feigned cough from Rick caught their attention.

"Would you care for some dessert?" asked the patient waitress.

"Oh, yes. Thank you, ma'am." Eldon & Ellen colored as they noticed Rick and Alise's twitching grins.

On the walk back to North Lawn, Eldon guided Ellen to a bench under a rose arbor. "Ellen, tonight has been very special. We have only two weeks until the semester ends. I know you need to attend Mississippi State this summer. When do you need to appear for registration?"

"MSU will be in session from June fifteenth to mid-August. Why do you ask?"

Eldon reached for her hand. "Ellen, I would like to introduce you to my family. Would you consider going with me to Indiana before returning to Mississippi?"

"I'd love to meet your family. But I'll need to alert my parents of a change in my arrival time. What would your parents think if you brought a friend home with you?" By now she hoped she was more than a friend.

"They were eager to meet you during spring break. Since that didn't work, I know they'll be more than happy to host you for a weekend. You can rest assured, they'll welcome you.

"I have a second motivation for this invitation. I think it will give both of us an opportunity to relate to each other in a nonacademic setting. I know I'll need to relinquish you to Lamar in your familiar home situation. I have just one request . . ." Eldon hesitated. Would he lose her by making his request? He decided it was a chance he'd need to take.

"Whatever it is, Eldon, I'll try to do what you ask." She looked at him with complete trust.

Her response gave him the courage he needed. "This may sound strange, but I'd like to request that you go home and date Lamar. Then make a decision as to who will have the privilege of loving you for a lifetime."

Ellen sucked in her breath. "That's a fair request. Believe me, I don't like the uncertainty any more than you do." She looked deeply into his eyes. "I'll go home and ask God to help me make the decision He would have me make regarding the future. Thank you for your gracious spirit in allowing me some time to think."

Eldon knew he was being a bit selfish. Yet he wanted to have one more weekend with Ellen before she returned to Lamar. He also wanted feedback from his parents, whose opinions were important to him.

Would Ellen be comfortable in a northern farm setting? Rosalie had been very uncomfortable. After Rosalie's visit, his father commented, "Son, Rosalie is a nice young lady. If you choose to marry her, Mom and I will do our best to learn to accept and love her. Just be aware; you come from two very different worlds. Perhaps God has someone else in store for you." His father's wise counsel had influenced Eldon's decision to end his relationship with Rosalie. Was Ellen the person God had been preparing to share his future?

Ellen's parents gave her their blessing to take an additional weekend to meet the Beacheys. After all, their families had intersected in previous generations. Her mother wrote, "We feel confident you will be received with warmth and mid-western hospitality."

Francis concluded her letter with, "Our friends, the Smuckers, will be returning to Missula after their vacation with northern Indiana relatives. Mary S. says they'll be more than happy to bring you back home." She included the Smucker's contact information.

Ellen didn't relish the task of alerting Lamar of the change in her arrival time. She picked up a piece of floral stationery and penned the missive.

Dear Lamar,

I've had a change of plans in my summer arrival date. From the very beginning of our friendship, we promised to be candid with each other. I've accepted Eldon Beachey's invitation to travel to Indiana to meet his family before returning home to Mississippi.

I hope this doesn't distress you too much. I feel I need to do this as part of my discernment process regarding my relationship with Eldon. Since I already know and appreciate your family, I trust you'll understand.

Sincerely,

Ellen

Lamar's reply came via airmail.

Dearest Ellen,

Your arrival was to have been fourteen more long days until you pulled into the Meridian train station. With your parents' permission, I had planned to meet you as you stepped off the Silver Bullet. Now I will need to wait four additional days before I get to see you again. It feels like Christmas was moved.

Do I understand your need to go to Indiana? Yes. In my head, it makes sense that you should meet Eldon's family. But in my heart, I would say, no, I don't understand.

Sincerely yours,

Lamar

Ellen was relieved once her return trip to Mississippi was arranged. But she still had qualms about meeting Eldon's parents.

"Alise, what if they don't like me or don't approve of me?" she asked one evening while taking a break from studying.

"I know they'll like you. If perchance they don't because of some quirk, you just turn on your irresistible southern charms, and they'll be captivated."

"You're no help. Go back to your studies."

"I thought I would." Alise laughed, ducking when Ellen threw a pillow in her direction.

End-of-the-school-year rides to Indiana came at a premium. Eldon was besieged with requests for transportation. The night before their six-hundred-mile trek, Eldon said, "There will be six of us leaving in the morning."

"You mean six young adults in one compact Corvair?"

Eldon grinned. "Do you mind? There'll be four girls in addition to us. It'll be cozy."

Ellen looked quizzical. "I don't mind being cozy, but where will we put luggage for five females traveling home for the summer?"

"Never fear. The smallest U-Haul trailer should solve the problem."

"Do you have any clue as to how much *stuff* five females can generate when going home for the summer?" She laughed. "I'll do my part to keep my luggage to a minimum and put the rest in school storage. That should help some."

"I think you're exaggerating. We'll be fine."

The next morning Eldon sized up each piece of luggage. He looked over at Ellen, who gave him an I-told-you-so look. Then with the eye of a mathematician and lots of determination, he began the process of packing the car trunk and U-haul trailer. As the final parcel fit into the trailer with a bit of persuasion, a cheer erupted from the girls. They were Indiana bound!

CHAPTER THIRTY-TWO

*H*aving delivered four female passengers to their destinations, Eldon and Ellen were finally alone. Eldon picked up speed for the final ten miles beyond the Shipshewana village limits. He turned onto a gravel road surrounded by acres of prairie farmland. Towering walnut and locust trees stood like sentinels along the roadside, creating a canopy of lush green branches.

Ellen laid a hand on Eldon's sleeve. Her gentle touch sent a tingle of excitement through his biceps. "What if your parents don't approve of me?" Her eyes mirrored her underlying apprehension.

His heart lurched. Wanting to allay her fear, Eldon drew her close in a one-armed embrace. "Ellen there's nothing about you to disapprove. Trust me. They'll be just as concerned that you approve of them."

"You think so?"

"I know so. . ." He squeezed her shoulder.

She relaxed against his protective arm.

In the gathering dusk, he could see her smile. *Lord, let this be the beginning of forever.*

Eldon liked the feel of being able to manage the car and trailer with one hand while keeping one arm around her shoulders. Within a mile, Eldon slowed the car to enter a wide gravel drive, coming to a stop by the sidewalk leading to the house. The typical mid-western white farmhouse had a front porch, ensconced in the midst of a neatly mown lawn.

On the left of the drive stood a white hip-roofed barn, large enough to accommodate a medium-sized dairy. Ellen caught sight of a bulk milk tank through the milk house windows. A cavernous haymow could swallow the year's crop of hay. Beside the barn, a towering silo took care of the cow's need for silage. A free-standing garage separated the farmhouse from the barn area. All the buildings were well maintained, an apparent trademark of the Beachey clan. This, at least, felt like a comfortable setting.

Before getting out of the car, he squeezed her hand. "You'll do just fine."

Skippy, Eldon's mixed-breed mutt, came bounding out to meet his master from his favorite spot near the back steps.

"Down boy, down." He ruffled the dog's fur while circling the car to open the door for Ellen.

Lee Beachey and Eldon's stepmother, Edna, emerged from the back door where they must have been keeping vigil from the kitchen window.

Lee gripped his son's hand. "Hello, Eldon, hello. Welcome home!"

Edna, stepped forward to shake Ellen's hand. "So, this is Eldon's friend." Her tone was warm and gracious.

Ellen wasn't quite sure what to make of their welcome. It was a bit different from her family where they would have been greeted with a bear hug from her father and enveloped in a gentle embrace from her mother. Both would have planted a kiss on her cheek.

Eldon said, "Dad and Mom, this is Ellen Yoder, most recently from Missula, Mississippi but grew up near Wausipi, Michigan. Her parents are Daniel and Francis Yoder." Eldon tried to create a frame of reference for his parents who valued connections with other Mennonite families.

"We're so pleased to meet you," Edna said. "Did your mother's family ever live near Thomas, Oklahoma?"

"Yes, that's where she met my father." Ellen didn't consider the question intrusive.

"When your mother's family moved to Oklahoma, they lived on a farm next to my family's farm. We enjoyed being neighbors."

"That's amazing. I knew my grandparents moved to Oklahoma for the sake of Grandma's health. She needed a drier climate than Michigan could provide."

"It's good to know where you come from," Lee added, "even though we've not had the privilege of knowing you. We'll try to remedy that situation this weekend. Welcome to our humble home, Ellen."

Edna led the way into the spacious farmhouse kitchen. She was an ample woman dressed in a homemade light green dress, a farm-wife floral apron, and a prayer covering. "I'll have supper ready in about ten minutes. Eldon, put Ellen's luggage in your sister's former bedroom." She appeared to be a take-charge woman.

Eldon whispered to Ellen, "Excuse me a minute. I'll be right back." He left to retrieve their luggage.

"Ellen, the bathroom is just around the corner to the left if you wish to use it before we eat. You'll find your belongings in the bedroom to your right at the top of the stairs." Edna gestured in the general direction of the stairway.

"Thank you. I won't be long."

Ellen retreated to the restroom and then to her designated bedroom. A spring breeze played with the blue dotted swiss curtains. White roller shades behind the semi-sheer panels could be lowered for privacy. Evidently, no wall decorations or pictures had been replaced since Eldon's sister Sara had taken all her personal belongings when she got married.

The bed was adorned with a hand-stitched blue dahlia patterned quilt, much like the quilts Ellen's mother created. The dresser with an attached mirror stood barren, except for a cool glass of water to welcome her which she enjoyed. At the foot of the bed sat a traditional cedar chest to store additional quilts. Eldon had placed her unopened suitcase on the cedar chest for easy access. A stuffed chair completed the furnishings.

Hmm, I can be comfortable here for the weekend. Glancing into the mirror, she noticed some *strubbles* had escaped from her usual coiffed appearance. Taking only a moment to tuck in the dark, wavy strands with a barrette, Ellen stepped out of the bedroom.

Across the hallway, leaning on the door jamb of his bedroom, Eldon waited. He smiled and closed the distance between them.

Taking both of her hands, he said, "They like you."

"How do you know?"

"I just know. You can relax."

Just then Edna called, "Supper's ready."

"Mom, we'll be right down."

Eldon took her hand as they skimmed down the steps. He gently seated Ellen to his right at the rectangular kitchen table. Seeing only four place settings, he frowned, "Where are David and James?"

"Oh, as soon as their evening chores were done, they left on a youth group bike hike. They'll be back late Sunday evening," Lee said.

"I thought it was awfully quiet around here." Eldon glanced at his father who winked. He wouldn't need to worry about the predictable teasing that Ellen's visit would have evoked from his two teenaged half-brothers.

Eldon glanced at the food on the table. "Thanks, Mom. This sure beats college food." He had noticed her efforts to please him and his guest. First impressions were important to his stepmother.

"You're welcome, Eldon."

The table was laden with Eldon's favorite foods: beef chunks smothered in savory gravy and served over noodles, a colorful mix of green and yellow beans, a tossed salad, homemade bread with strawberry jam, and Dutch apple pie. Besides the growing friendship of the young lady seated next to him, what more could he possibly want?

Early Saturday morning, Ellen awakened to familiar farm sounds wafting through her bedroom window. She smiled at the sound of chickens squawking the birth of a new day into her consciousness. Cows mooed in their stanchions. Glancing at her alarm clock, she was startled to see it was six o'clock. How had she slept so long when life on a dairy farm began at five?

Springing out of bed, she slipped into a casual dress that could get dirty without duress. She would help with any chores that still needed to be done, especially since Eldon's younger brothers were gone for the weekend.

She found Edna in the kitchen preparing a farmer's breakfast of fried mush, tomato gravy and sausage patties. The aroma made Ellen's stomach growl in anticipation.

"Edna, do you mind if I go out to help with any chores that haven't been done?"

"I don't mind at all, but you're our guest. You needn't feel obligated."

"I don't feel obligated. I'm just embarrassed that I overslept. I assumed I would help just like I would if I were home.

Ellen lost no time passing through the milk-house with its gleaming stainless-steel bulk tank. Cocking her head around the door into the milking area, she called, "Good Morning," hoping to be heard above the loud hissing suction of milking machines.

She could see Eldon and his father emerging from the broad sides of black and white Holstein cows. With milkers in hand, they quickly emptied milk into waiting stainless-steel buckets then positioned the milkers on the next cows.

Both stopped in mid-stride, replying in tandem, "Good Morning."

Eldon's muscles rippled beneath a dark green tee shirt as he strode toward her, carrying heavy-buckets of milk without effort. "What brings you out at this hour into this smelly barn?" His wide grin betrayed his delight at her appearance.

She raised an eyebrow. "You, of course. But I thought I'd help with the chores since your brothers aren't here. Have the eggs been gathered?"

"Ah, no, they haven't been, but we weren't expecting you to do it."

"I'd be happy to gather the eggs if you'll show me where to find the baskets."

Eldon's father stepped up next to Ellen. "Young lady, you don't have to do this. Sometimes those clucks are a bit feisty in the morning."

She giggled. "I know. As an eight-year-old, my job was to gather eggs before getting ready for school. Hens squawk a lot as if to say, 'You can't make me give up my eggs, but I can be persuaded.'"

"Son, she understands chickens. Show her where to find that hen house. We'll take all the help we can get this morning."

After orienting Ellen to the chicken house of a hundred laying hens, Eldon jogged back to the barn grinning from ear to ear. *What a difference from Rosalie's visit.*

Stooping to attach four milker cups to the teats of the next Holstein, he felt his father's hand on his shoulder. He looked up to see Lee's gentle smile of approval.

"Son, I don't know what you're waiting for, but I think this is your match."

"I think you're right, Dad. All I need to do is to convince her." His face clouded. "If only I didn't need to send her back to Lamar this summer."

"I know it's hard. But don't rush her. You want Ellen to be just as convinced as you are."

Eldon nodded. Sometimes doing the right thing was the hardest thing to do.

Saturday evening, before the two were ready to retire to their separate bedrooms, Eldon said, "Ellen, I have a small gift for you."

"A gift? I wasn't anticipating a gift. I didn't bring one for you."

"Don't worry. Your visit is my gift from you."

He opened a bag, producing a pink gift-wrapped package. For one unaccustomed to buying gifts, he hoped she wouldn't be offended or displeased. He dared not breathe as she un-wrapped it with deft hands.

Her eyes grew wide and she uttered a joyous, "Oh! I've always wanted a copy of Oswald Chamber's devotional *My Utmost for His Highest*. I'll think of you whenever I read it." She touched the cover with reverence.

He chuckled. "I'd better confess my sins. I was hoping it would encourage you spiritually this summer, plus prompt you to think of me when you're far away in Mississippi."

She laughed at his unabashed confession. "You're forgiven."

Ellen wasn't sure what to think when Edna introduced her at church as Eldon's girlfriend. Not that she minded being Eldon's girlfriend. Her face turned crimson and her pulse quickened at the thought. It's just that she wasn't ready to make a public declaration. After all, he hadn't asked her to go steady yet. She thought she knew what she wanted, but was that what God wanted? Where did Lamar and foreign missions fit in this mix?

Sunday afternoon was gorgeous with bright sunshine and seventy-five-degree weather. Fetching two lawn chairs and tall glasses of fresh lemonade, the couple gravitated to a grassy spot under a nearby maple tree.

Seated next to each other their forearms touched for a second, a hint of electricity jolted her. Feeling her face flush, she stole a glance at Eldon only to find laugh lines twitching at the corner of his lips.

"What are you thinking, Mr. Beachey?"

"What am I thinking? I am thinking it's pretty special to be seated next to one of the most beautiful young women I have ever met, especially when she blushes."

She changed the subject. "Have you decided what you'll do this summer?"

They'd been so pre-occupied with sharing childhood experiences, family dynamics, likes, dislikes, and God's call on their future plans, they hadn't talked about the immediate. Or perhaps they had avoided the immediate.

"I've checked with my previous factory foreman, and I can go back to Starcraft to work with metal on the night shift while attending summer school at Goshen College." He took a sip of lemonade. "How about you? Do you plan to work at Missula General while attending Mississippi State?"

She shook her head. "Since I need to commute an hour to MSU, my class schedule won't allow me to put in the required eight-hour shifts at the hospital. But I've agreed to do some private duty nursing, and I'll work some evenings at Missula Bookstore for Mrs. Harris who is a real sweetheart."

"Will that be enough to cover your costs at MSU?"

"I'm afraid not." She looked away, embarrassed to admit her lack of finances. "I'll be able to earn enough to cover transportation and texts, but tuition will need to come from a student loan from our local bank," she said.

Her face brightened as their talk drifted to other safer subjects.

Early Monday morning, Ellen needed to meet the Smuckers for the long trip home. The weekend had been too short—way too short. Ellen was quiet as the little white Corvair began eating up the fifteen miles to the pick-up point.

Eldon struggled to say a thousand words that just didn't seem appropriate. *I think we can survive the summer but what if— just what if that Lamar guy sweeps her off her feet. Lord, I can't bear to lose her. Not now, not ever.*

Eldon reached for her hand that seemed so small within his. "Ellen, I think you know that I care a lot about you. But I won't hem you in. I want you to go home to decide whether your future includes me or Lamar."

Her eyes welled up with unshed tears. "And I have come to care for you. I just wish I knew what God already knows. . . which way I should take." Her voice trembled.

"While you sort it out, I would like to suggest we write to each other every day since neither one of us has the money to call," he said.

"I like that idea. Can't you just see our rural mail carriers shaking their heads in amazement?" There was that Southern accent again accompanied by her impish grin.

"Thank you for introducing me to your parents. It's been a delight to see you interact with your parents. I felt comfortable and welcomed."

"I'm glad you enjoyed it. As y'all say, I was "right proud" to have you as my guest. I'm certain my parents feel the same."

"Would you consider coming to Mississippi sometime this summer to meet my family?'

"That sounds like a neat idea. Maybe I can manage to come at the end of summer school. I'd like to meet your parents,"

Reaching their destination, he parked the car. Taking both of her hands in his, he said, "Let's pray. Father, we trust you will show each of us and Lamar the way you want us to go. We entrust our future into your hands. Protect Ellen while we are separate from each other and as she travels home with the Smuckers. In Jesus' name I pray. Amen."

After stowing her two suitcases in the back of the Smucker station wagon, he drew her into a side hug. With his free hand, he reached into the inner pocket of his spring jacket. "Here is the first installment of my summer letters. Just be sure to wait to open it until you get home. Promise?"

She looked quizzical. With a tentative smile, she said, "I promise. And I'll write as soon as I get to Pop and Mom's. You can count on it."

Within minutes, the Smuckers were loaded and ready to leave. Then with a wave, she was gone. He watched until the blue station wagon negotiated the turn at the end of the drive where trees blocked his view. Walking toward his car, silence reverberated around him. How could the absence of one little lady create such a hollow space within him?

CHAPTER THIRTY-THREE

llen slipped the white security envelope into her purse. She could feel its thickness and wondered what it contained. Had he written a five-page letter giving her an ultimatum that she terminate her relationship with Lamar within a week or two? That was unlike Eldon. He had told her she should go home to sort out her feelings. How could she sort them out if she had no opportunity to date Lamar?

What was in that envelope? To avoid arousing any suspicion from the Smuckers, Ellen would touch the envelope whenever she "needed" a Kleenex or pencil or any other item in her well-stocked purse. Sometimes the envelope served as tangible evidence of Eldon's presence. At other times, she itched to open it. But she wouldn't renege on a promise.

The highway went on and on without end, meandering through the full length of Indiana. Then the loaded station wagon labored up and down the lush hills of Kentucky and Tennessee. Fifteen hours passed before the headlights flashed onto the "Welcome to Mississippi" sign.

Five-year-old Justin Smucker couldn't contain his joy. His little-boy tenor belted out verse one of the hymn, "Hallelujah, what a Savior."

Ellen and the senior Smuckers laughed. "Son, we say 'Hallelujah' too," Mr. Smucker said. "Especially since Jesus is our Savior. He's protecting us on this long trip. It'll only be a couple more hours until we're home."

"Okay, Daddy." Justin and his two younger siblings fell asleep again.

Sleep bypassed Ellen. At two a. m., the car tires crunched on the gravel driveway of the Yoder home. Mom's welcome light was still burning in the living room. She could see lights flicker in her parents' bedroom window. They must have been listening for her return.

Ellen almost wept with relief and weariness. Keeping her emotions in check, she turned to her travel hosts. "Thanks so much for being willing to provide transportation for me. You have been very gracious."

"It's been our pleasure," Mrs. Smucker said. "Thank you for all the stories you read to the children and for entertaining them with road games."

By the time Mr. Smucker unloaded Ellen's luggage, her father appeared. He gave his daughter a quick hug, then turned to Mr. Smucker. "Thank you so much for bringing our *glenne Betsy* back to us." He handed a check to Mr. Smucker for Ellen's travel expenses.

"You are welcome. We considered it a privilege," Mr. Smucker said.

As the Smucker vehicle exited the drive, Ellen stumbled into her mother's arms.

"It's so good to be home," she whispered. She didn't want to awaken her younger brother.

"It's good to have you back home. We'll talk in the morning, once you've had some sleep. Sleep as long as you wish. Pop already put your luggage in your bedroom. Goodnight."

Fatigue washed over her entire being. Ellen closed her bedroom door. She had to know what was in that envelope from Eldon. Her hands shook as she ripped open the seal. A note encased a wad of bills.

Dearest Ellen,

I hope it's permissible to call you "dearest" because that is what you have become to me. I asked that you wait to read this note until you had some privacy. It was a special privilege to have you visit my home. My parents enjoyed getting to know you which I was certain they would. How could they not like you?

Eldon sounded like Alise. She continued to read, her heart pounding furiously.

During our conversations, I gathered you would struggle to meet the tuition costs of MSU. I'm not sure of the exact amount of the tuition but thought this might lessen the need for a student loan for summer school.

Please accept my gift to you because I care.

Much love,

Eldon

Ellen sank down on the edge of the bed. Breathless, she counted the ten and twenty-dollar bills, and even a fifty. She burst into tears. *Lord, it's the exact amount I need for my tuition. Eldon's love for me and your provision is over whelming. Thank ya' Jesus!*

She climbed into bed with the sound of crickets lulling her to sleep.

CHAPTER THIRTY-FOUR

L amar waited one agonizing additional day to call Ellen, giving her the opportunity to get some much-needed sleep.

Today was her first day of summer school at MSU. His fingers tapped the phone stand as he waited for Mrs. Yoder to call Ellen to the phone.

"Hello," came the voice he'd longed to hear.

"Hello, Ellen. Welcome home." His stomach refused to be calm.

"Thanks, Lamar. It's so good to be home."

"Can we get together this evening?" He hoped she couldn't hear the longing in his voice.

"Lamar, I'm not trying to be difficult, but my professors are expecting us to cover a semesters' worth of material in three weeks. I came home today loaded with assignments. Would Friday evening work? I'd like to be free to enjoy our time together rather than knowing I'm jeopardizing my grades."

"I've been to summer school before, so I understand the courses are concentrated. The first day of classes can be brutal. Right now, I wish I didn't understand. I was so hoping to see you tonight, but Friday evening will be okay." He bit his lip to keep from saying something he'd regret.

"I'm sorry Lamar. I do appreciate your understanding."

Never one to brood, he brightened. "I'd like to pick you up at six-thirty. We can eat at Boykins then drive out to the Bluff."

"I'll look forward to it."

He would too.

Friday evening finally came, and Lamar couldn't contain his excitement. As he escorted Ellen to the car, he stepped lighter than usual.

They eased out onto the highway.

She turned to him. "Lamar, in your last letter you indicated that you weren't feeling good. Have you been really sick? You do look like you've lost some weight."

He wiggled his eyebrows and blinked. A grin tugged at his lips. "I thought I could hide it from my little nurse. I might have known you'd detect it. I guess y'all could say I've been really sick for about two weeks. Dr. Percy says it was some tropical bug I picked up in the Congo. He pronounced me cured earlier this week. He predicts it will not recur. Now that you're back, I am totally well."

He beamed as he reached for her hand. She blushed.

Same night, Eleven p.m.

Dear Eldon,

Summer school at MSU in Starkville, Mississippi, is a far cry from EMC. The university is huge. You could place several EMCs in the midst of this campus. So far, I've been at the right place at the right time.

To insure the continued implementation of campus desegregation, we have National Guardsmen everywhere except in the ladies' bathrooms. They would probably be in our restrooms, if they had female Guards. Thus far, integration at MSU has been the most peaceful of all the southern colleges where black students have enrolled.

The presence of the National Guard doesn't frighten me. I'm just grateful that MSU upholds the US policy that everyone, regardless of race or ethnicity, deserves a quality education.

You asked that I tell you what happened during my time with Lamar. I couldn't bring myself to cast a shadow on his obvious happiness. But I know I can't go on without telling him more about you and me.

He asked to see me again tomorrow evening because he is working as an Assistant Camp Director. Youth camp begins the next day which is Sunday. This means he will be on duty around the clock. I doubt I'll see much of him for the next two weeks.

I plan to tell him tomorrow evening that you will be coming down later this summer. If he wants to keep dating, even though he knows I am also interested in someone else, I feel I can't say no right away. I'm confused. We're just not tuned into the same wave length. I do like him a lot, but it stops there.

Sincerely,
Ellen

Two weeks later an afternoon rain washed away the day's humidity. Lamar and Ellen walked toward the picnic area as a refreshing early evening breeze tousled her hair. A touch of pine fragrance mingled with the heavier scent of magnolias. The pine needle path meandered along the edge of the impressive Tombigbee River where a commercial barge bellowed its approach to an oncoming fishing boat.

Ellen felt like summer in a mint green, lace-trimmed, A-line dress that highlighted her slim silhouette and dark brown hair.

With picnic basket in one hand and Ellen's hand in the other, Lamar guided them to a quiet spot on a cliff overlooking the deep blue waters of the mighty river. He deposited the basket on a picnic table, and turned to her.

"Ellen, you're beautiful tonight."

"Thank you, Lamar." A flush crept across her cheeks. If only he didn't look at her with such undisguised adoration. She dreaded the thought of snuffing out that light in his eyes.

"You're welcome." He relinquished her hand. "Let's see what you packed in this basket. I'm starved after running all day to keep up with juvenile campers. We can talk while we eat."

Ellen spread a red plaid cloth on the table and unpacked utensils, coordinating plates, cups and ample containers of food. Then they slid into seats across from each other.

"What a treat! Southern fried chicken, potato salad, vegetables, dip, chips, sweetened iced tea and apple pie. After surviving on Congolese food for three years, this is soul food."

They both laughed.

"Ellen, one thing I appreciate about you is that you do things that are inexpensive. Thanks for volunteering to prepare this feast."

"I assumed that since both of us are saving every possible penny for next year's tuition, it makes sense to keep costs at a minimum."

With a slow shake of his head, he chuckled. "You amaze me."

Their conversation revolved around college assignments and the antics of campers before turning to more serious subjects. Lamar's face was animated as he described the aviation courses being offered by Moody Bible Institute.

"I can't wait for September to begin," he said. Then his face sobered. "There's just one down side to attending Moody. It'll put even more distance between you and me when you go back East for the fall semester. Have you thought anymore about foreign missions?"

She nodded. Looking down at her plate, she pushed a morsel of apple pie in an aimless circle. "I've been thinking every spare moment."

She met his gaze. "Lamar, before coming to Mississippi two years ago, I was positive the Lord was calling me into foreign missions."

"And now?" He leaned back as though fearing her answer.

She looked out over the water with unseeing eyes. "And now I'm not sure," her voice trickled to a mere whisper. She glanced back at him, anguish in her heart. "Today I understand that no matter where I serve—state-side or abroad—my first assignment is to be an ambassador for Christ."

He nodded, trying to understand what she was about to say.

"If I'm reading your question correctly," she continued, "my second assignment seems to be to discern whether I'm to carry out that calling with you in a foreign setting or with Eldon somewhere in the U.S." With a wry grin she added, "Wouldn't it be great if God wrote the answer in the spongy mud down at the water's edge?"

"I'll be more than happy to help God along."

Their laughter diffused their pain.

He grew pensive. "On second thought, I'll let God's spirit whisper his answer to your heart. Just keep me posted because I believe he wants both of us to be in his will."

She sat up straight. A burden had lifted from her shoulders. "Lamar, thanks for your gracious attitude. I do need to tell you that as part of the discernment process, Eldon plans to come for a weekend to meet my family later this summer. I would like to wait until that time to make a decision. If you prefer to cut off our relationship tonight in light of that visit, I'll understand."

"I've had the fortunate opportunity to get to know you and your family. He should have the same privilege. I'll take my chances," he said.

She mused silently. A lot of women don't get the chance to meet such an understanding, caring guy. I've met two and I thank God for both of their willingness to not push me into a premature decision.

Eleven p.m.

Dear Eldon,

As I promised, tonight I told Lamar about your proposed trip to Mississippi. He wants to keep on seeing me in spite of your up-coming visit. It's as though he's hoping God will change my mind.

Am I turning a deaf ear to the plan God has for me? What am I to say? I've agreed to date him, but he understands there will be limits.

Sincerely yours,
Ellen

Dearest Ellen,

Thank you for alerting Lamar that I plan to come see you at the end of summer school. Are you turning a deaf ear to God's plan for your life? I don't think so.

If I'm reading God's plan correctly for my life, it always includes you.

It would be so helpful if we had the money to finance long-distance phone calls. Each letter makes me wish I had the next one. This feels like the mystery stories I used to read while growing up. The only problem with this plot is that I'm one of the characters. The outcome will make the difference of a lifetime for you, for me, and for Lamar. I'm trying to turn everything over to God and to trust him for the outcome.

Lest you have any doubts as to my family's assessment, Mom let me know before you left that she approved of you and our relationship. She has reiterated those sentiments several times since your weekend with us.

Dad was a bit more reserved. Saturday morning, we were working together in the barn. I asked point blank, "Dad, what do you think about my relationship with Ellen?"

Without hesitation he said, "From what I've observed, I approve one-hundred per cent. It would be easy to accept her into the family."

Of course, I agree! I think Dad doesn't want me to pressure you. I do want you to be as convinced as I am. But it's hard to wait.

With love,
Eldon

CHAPTER THIRTY-FIVE

*L*amar eked out a few moments from his camp administrative duties to call Ellen. He had to make every opportunity count before Eldon got there. He wet his lips, and ran a hand through his hair.

The phone rang

"Good afternoon, Yoders, Ellen speaking."

He rubbed the back of his neck. "Good afternoon to y'all. Ellen, the Choctaw festival is in session. I have Friday evening free. Would you like to attend with me?" He paced, hoping she wouldn't be too snowed in with assignments to accept his invitation. Each year it was held at the Choctaw reservation in Philadelphia, Mississippi.

"What a thoughtful invitation. I'd enjoy going to the fair with you. I've never attended this important Choctaw event. Besides, I'd welcome the relief from World Literature."

He relaxed. "There will be a stickball tournament, and the Choctaw Indian princess pageant is scheduled for Friday evening. We should leave at five o'clock. Don't eat supper. There'll be plenty of tribal food available."

"Thanks. I'll look forward to seeing you at five."

He hung up the phone.

The camp director walked into the office. "I take it the phone call went well."

"Couldn't have been better!"

His boss slapped Lamar a high five.

Ellen sat at the dining room table, bent over her textbooks, sometimes sighing deeply, sometimes staring off into space. She got up and went to the kitchen to get a tall glass of mint tea. Retracing her steps to the table, she sank back into her chair. Her eyes connected with her mother's, who had been busy nearby at her quilting frame.

Francis came to the end of a long row of tiny stitches which created linking hearts on the wide white border of a quilt. "I wasn't trying to eavesdrop, but I couldn't help hearing your conversation with Lamar. Did that call distress you?"

Ellen's eyes were bright with unshed tears. "Yes and no. I'm sure we'll have a good time together at the festival. I just wish I knew where God wanted me." She rubbed her forehead. "Oh, Mom, I just want to be able to come to love either Eldon or Lamar with my whole heart, not just half of it."

Her mother nodded. "I understand. I've been trying to remain neutral and not meddle with your decision. It's been difficult for my mothers' heart to watch you vacillate between two upstanding young men of integrity. I believe either could be a good husband for you."

She looked deeply into Ellen's eyes. "Perhaps it's time that I share our story." She stopped to re-thread her needle. "Your father and I began dating in Oklahoma during our late teens. Mother had died two years earlier, and my father decided to move back to Michigan where our extended family lived. Even though I didn't want to leave my boyfriend, I had no choice. I needed to go with my family to care for my six younger siblings. Father remarried a year later."

"So how did you stay in touch with Pop?" Ellen had never heard this part of her parents' story.

"Before my family left, your father asked for permission to write to me. With great anticipation, I looked forward to our postman's deliveries." A smile tugged at Mother's lips at the long-ago memory.

"How long did it take for a letter to reach you all the way from Oklahoma?"

"Two weeks," her mother answered.

"Two weeks! Sometimes three days seems like an eternity when I'm waiting on a letter from Eldon." Ellen would go crazy if she had to wait that long for a letter.

Mother nodded and chuckled. "I didn't know whether my relationship with your Poppa would flourish or flounder. While waiting for your father to declare himself, I occasionally dated several other young men. That only served to complicate the issue for me. In time, I decided to sever all ties with others. A year later, the very best letter arrived in which your father asked me to marry him."

Ellen gasped. "You mean you hadn't seen each other for a whole year? Yet, when he proposed by letter, you accepted?"

"I did."

"In addition to working fulltime on your grandparents' farm, your father picked cotton to earn money for my train fare back to Oklahoma. We were married two weeks later. Eleven children and forty-five years later, I've not been one bit sorry.

Ellen, your father and I have tried not to interfere in your affairs. You're an adult, but may I make a suggestion?" her mother stopped.

"Sure. Go ahead."

"It may be alright for you to get to know Lamar. Just don't wait so long to make up your mind that you get all befuddled regarding your feelings for Eldon."

"Thanks, Mom, for sharing your story and for your input. I'll give it some serious thought."

CHAPTER THIRTY-SIX

*M*ississippi paraded a gorgeous summer day. Ellen
dressed with unusual care. She adjusted the belt of the
white ruffled apron over her deep blue Choctaw
dress. At last, she would get to wear Shonia's
masterpiece. Hearing Lamar's car tires on the gravel drive, she
snapped the delicate beaded necklace in place.

The knock at the door beckoned her. She opened it with a
welcoming, "Do come in."

Lamar stepped over the threshold. "I can't believe it. My very
own Choctaw princess!"

She beamed in spite of herself. "I'm not so sure about the
princess part, but I do have the festival costume, thanks to
Shonia. Before I left for college, she made this for me. It was a

thank you for teaching her introductory English. Shonia says all the intricate half-diamond appliqués on this skirt, bodice, and apron, represent the eastern diamondback rattlesnake."

For a brief second, Lamar touched her necklace which formed a half diamond pattern. She flushed at his nearness.

He leaned back against the door frame. "Ellen, you do justice to the outfit. If the pageant were open to Caucasians, I'm sure you'd win." His smile lit up his whole face. "Are you ready to go? I know you'll enjoy the fair."

Ellen agreed. She'd looked forward to this day.

En-route to the festival, Ellen plied Lamar with questions. "Lamar, you grew up surrounded by the Choctaw culture. My exposure has been quite limited. Can you tell me what to expect tonight?"

"We'll be in time for the stickball tournament. It's been part of their culture for hundreds of years. In early American history, the game outcome was sometimes used to settle disputes. Today it's become a symbol of tribal identity. Each player has *kabotcha* which are two carved hickory sticks with a leather cup on the end in which players carry and catch the *towa* or ball. Tonight is the playoff of this fast-moving sport."

Lamar winked at her. "Any other questions, Miss Mennonite Choctaw?'

"Yes, tell me about the Indian Princess pageant, please."

"Well, I'm more familiar with stickball, but I'm told the princess must be between the ages of sixteen and nineteen. A panel of judges awards points to each contestant based on her communication skills, poise, traditional dress, personality, and cultural understanding. The princess then becomes a goodwill ambassador for the Choctaws at tribal events. She's a key figure in helping preserve their culture."

"Hmm—the panel of judges for the Miss USA pageant should take a few lessons from the Choctaws." Ellen turned to face Lamar. "I do have another question."

"Yes?"

"Ever since you invited me I've been thinking about Shonia. Do you think we might see her and Will tonight?"

"You really miss Shonia, don't you?' Lamar looked straight down the road so she couldn't read his expression.

She nodded, pursing her lips while scanning the horizon. "I had hoped to see her when I came home for the summer. Mother told me they left the Missula area to be closer to Will's family at Pine Ridge. Shonia left no forwarding address, so we've lost touch. . ." her voice faded.

He reached for her hand and squeezed it. "Thousands of people will be at the fair. If we don't see them tonight, I'll make sure you get to see her before either of us leave for school this fall."

"Thanks." She smiled her gratitude.

When Lamar and Ellen arrived, the fairground was teeming with cars and pedestrians. Lamar looked like he knew precisely where he was going. He parked with ease near the entrance of gate twelve.

Ellen scrutinized the crowd. Her mouth fell open. She grabbed his arm. "Lamar, is that who I think it is?"

Emerging from the vehicle ahead of them were four familiar figures. Ellen forgot to wait for Lamar to open the car door for her. She jumped out of the car in a flash.

Embracing her friend, she cried. "Shonia, is it really you?"

Shonia hugged her like she wouldn't let her go. The two friends laughed and cried at the same time.

"It's me and Will and Missy and Willette."

Ellen's heart melted. "Your daughters are growing up."

Everyone exchanged greetings. Ellen looked at Lamar who stood two feet away with his arms crossed and a self-satisfied grin.

She flashed him an ever-widening smile that bubbled into a giggle. "Lamar, y'all planned this didn't you?"

He opened his hands as though releasing what had been hidden. "It's 'fess-up time. Am I forgiven?"

She laughed. "You are so bad, but you're forgiven." What a wonderful surprise that he'd done this for her. She'd never expected Lamar to arrange something so close to her heart. She had to hold back her tears. Pulling herself together, she changed the subject. "Now, there are things to do and sights to see. Where do we go from here?"

"Will, would you and Shonia lead the way?" Lamar asked. "You know what's happening where and when."

The Choctaw couple led the group toward the fair midway.

Shy Willette slipped her hand in Ellen's and whispered, "I like your dress. You look like us."

Ellen bent to give the little girl a hug and whispered, "I like looking like you."

The Tatums were in full tribal regalia. Shonia's crimson, floor-length dress and Will's matching shirt were trimmed with full diamond rattlesnake designs. Four beaded medallions marched down the front of Will's shirt. His black felt hat sported a band of hand-crafted red and white diamonds. Twelve-year-old Missy and ten-year-old Willette's outfits matched Ellen's half diamond trim. Shonia had outdone herself in creating full diamond necklaces for each of her family.

Shonia cocked her head to check out Ellen's appearance. "When you're wearing my dress, you look like a Choctaw."

"And you sound like an English lady. Your English is flawless," Ellen said.

Will walked ahead, chest thrust out. His shoulders back. He beamed. The reserved husband proclaimed, "My Shonia speak good English. She work hard. Soon a teacher."

"A teacher?" Ellen raised an eyebrow as she looked to Shonia for clarification.

"I've applied for a job in the school system as a teaching assistant. Yesterday I had my second interview, and they told me I have been given a position. I want to help children learn English just as you helped me. Yet they must be able to speak their mother tongue too."

"Shonia, I may have helped you begin the process of speaking English, but you persevered. I'm right proud of you."

The two men walked in sync. "Will," Lamar ventured, "tell us about your new job. I see you're driving a car. How did that happen?"

"God good." Will's eyes glistened. "Pine Ridge job, Mennonite Farmer Miller. Make me boss-man, no—" He looked at Shonia, puzzled.

"Foreman," she said.

"Yes, foreman. He own five-hundred acres. He teach tractor, car. We farm beans. Mr. Miller give car, part of pay. No more chop cotton. Yes!"

Laughter rippled through the party of six as they reached the midway.

Ellen couldn't be prouder of her protégé and her family. God had truly been good to them.

The *ahilpa chitos* military style snare drums signaled the opening of the dance performances. Missy and Willette found their places in the children's ring. Their dance mimicked the behavior of little animals. With joyful dance steps, they darted in and out of the ring like playful raccoons, circling to the applause of watching adults.

"Come," Shonia said. "You must see the happiest dance. The *ahilpa chitos* are calling Will and me. Missy and Willette stay here with Lamar and Ellen. We will return at the close of the dance."

An immense crowd gathered around the dance arena, and Ellen and Lamar vied to get a good spot where they could see the dancers clearly. They kept a watchful eye on the two little girls while Will and Shonia slipped into place as dancers.

The dancers moved to the rise and fall of a chanter's voice, who kept time by striking together a pair of sticks.

"Lamar, do you know what this dance means? Sometimes they move slowly, sometimes in rapid rhythm." Ellen was enthralled with the flawless choreography.

Lamar nodded. "This is a social dance marking the important aspects of friendship, courtship, and marriage. Watch the expression on their faces as the warrior asks for the hand of his beloved."

Will and Shonia seemed to be reliving their romantic past, and it touched Ellen's heart. She hoped that someday she too would be able to show such genuine affection for a man.

Dancing beside them, a young couple portrayed the radiance of a recent engagement and marriage. Ellen was certain she'd seen the face of the girl before, but where and when?

The dance culminated with the exhilarating wedding scene of "jumping over the stick." The beautiful young couple stepped out of the dance circle in front of Lamar and Ellen. The girl tossed back her luxurious jet-black hair.

"Rena Westin!" Ellen called to her, as the young lady moved toward her.

Rena grasped Ellen's hands. "Ms. Yoder," she exclaimed, excitement dancing in her face."Wesley, this is the nurse that helped me in my darkest hour." Awe embroidered her voice.

"*Ya gogay*, Ms. Yoder for my beautiful Rena." He looked at the ground, possibly unaccustomed to addressing a white woman.

Rena looked radiant. "I'm no longer Rena Westin. I'm now Mrs. Wesley Watashe, of Crystal Ridge. We've been married two months." Wesley's love must've contributed to a stunning transformation in Rena.

The crowd milled around them. Rena drew Ellen aside for a moment. "Baby Marie Ellen is okay?"

Ellen nodded. "The Hershbergers tell me she is well loved and cared for in her adoptive home. That's all I know."

Rena blinked away a sudden spat of tears. "*Ya gogay*. Thank you. I will be happy knowing she is happy."

"You can rest knowing she is being loved with the love of Jesus," Ellen said.

Rena threw her arms around her in a tight embrace. Then with a wave, she and Wesley disappeared into the crowd.

Thank you, Lord, for providing Rena with a good husband. She looks radiant and well cared for. All around her, Ellen was surrounded by couples in love. An ache formed in her heart. Would it ever be her turn?

Once the dance had ended, Missy and Willette scampered off with their parents.

Lamar and Ellen stopped by some food stands where vendors offered the Choctaw favorite of hominy in huge black iron pots cooked over open fires. Southern fried chicken and frybread along with hominy made for a savory meal, even though it wasn't the most nutritious.

Finding a grassy spot, the couple sat down to enjoy their feast. "How long have you known that young lady dancer?"

"I didn't introduce you because of privacy issues. Lamar, that young lady is the girl who helped integrate Missula General Hospital."

"She must be a remarkable young woman. I'm glad she seems to be doing so well after such a traumatic experience."

"You don't know how often I've prayed for her. I'm so glad she's doing so well."

Reverberating drums summoned them to the stickball playoff. Players had exchanged their native garb for tee shirts, blue jeans and bare feet. The Mississippi team was pitted against the Oklahoma contingent.

"Lamar, you'll need to fill me in. I haven't the foggiest idea of what's happening."

Seeking to be heard above the noise of the crowd around them, Lamar leaned toward her. Their shoulders touched, sending heat waves through-out his body. Was she aware of what her nearness did to him? He forced himself to concentrate on answering her request.

"I'll try to explain as we go along," he said. "Stickball is a variation of lacrosse. The two teams try to propel the *towa*—woven ball— toward their designated goal posts with the help of their cupped hickory sticks."

A moan erupted from the Oklahoma fans. "What happened?" she asked.

"The Oklahoma player touched the ball with his hands—the equivalent of a foul. Watch. The *towa* is back in the Mississippi court. They've scored a goal!" Lamar jumped to his feet and he and the crowd went wild.

The teams were well matched for speed and agility. In the final drum roll, the Mississippi Band of Choctaws was declared the national Stickball Champions.

"What a tournament!" Ellen cried. "I see what you mean when you say this is a fast-moving game. Part of the time I couldn't even tell which team had the *towa*."

Lamar laughed. "Neither could I. We just hope the referees are fast enough to keep up with the speed of the team."

They evacuated the stands with the rest of the crowd, Lamar being sure to not let go of Ellen so as not to become separated.

"The final event of the day is about to begin. If we hurry we won't miss the Indian Princess Pageant." Lamar led Ellen to a choice seat near the front of the observation bleachers.

The stage floor was covered with red carpeting. Strings of overhead lights swayed in a mid-summer breeze. Beautiful romantic music introduced the pageant. Each potential princess walked on stage in her exquisite tribal dress and jewelry, basking in the applause of the crowd.

Judges posed questions that highlighted a contestant's cultural knowledge. At the end of a long evening, the final points were tallied and the 1967 Choctaw Indian Princess was presented to a cheering crowd.

As Lamar and Ellen walked to the car, she observed, "Tonight's princess is more than a beauty queen. She is a beautiful, intelligent young woman who is also poised and engaging."

Lamar nodded. "I agree. She'll do an excellent job of representing the tribe in the coming year whether it's on the local, state or national level."

Although, he thought the true princess sat beside him now.

Approaching the lighted front entrance of the Yoder residence, Ellen looked up at Lamar. "Thank you for a wonderful evening. It was all I anticipated and more. I enjoyed our time together. And thanks so much for orchestrating the surprise meeting with Will and Shonia and their girls. Then seeing Rena's happiness with Wesley was a bonus."

Lamar savored the sparkle in her eyes and the flush on her face. He ached to kiss her goodnight, but she had made it clear she'd wait to kiss the man she'd marry. "It's been a great evening for me too. I'll call as soon as I'm given my schedule for the next few weeks. Good night, my little Mennonite Princess."

"Goodnight, Lamar."

Inching his way out the drive, his last glimpse in the rearview mirror was of a petite Choctaw Princess silhouetted in the doorway of the Yoder residence. Would he be able to win her heart or had her Yankee suitor become all Lamar hoped he'd be to her?

CHAPTER THIRTY-SEVEN

Eldon was exhausted as he sat down to write another letter. If only he could see Ellen or talk to her. A long-distance phone call to iron out a thorny issue was out of the question. One did not place a long-distance call for personal reasons.

I'm going to help her decide. He picked up his pen. It was his last paragraph that packed a punch.

11:30 p. m., Thursday evening

> *Dear Ellen,*
>
> *. . . You say that Lamar seems to hope against hope that you'll change your mind. Have you not made up your*

mind? Or are you using him to keep from loneliness? Let me remind you that once you've come to a conclusion, the sooner that decision is made known, the easier it will be for everyone involved.

Love,

Eldon

This letter should reach her on Monday. He slept soundly for the first time in weeks.

Saturday morning, Eldon had a reprieve from his grueling schedule. He was working full-time on the night shift at a local factory, attending summer school at Goshen College, and helping his father on the farm. Plowing, planting, and harvesting had become a welcome release for pent-up emotions as he awaited Ellen's decision.

I should be feeling relieved. I told her what I thought. Lord, what if I did the wrong thing and pushed her into the arms of Lamar? This morning he'd volunteered to clean out the barnyard. He shoveled several scoops then leaned on the shovel handle, lost in thought. Progress was slow. His shoulders drooped. The whole world looked gray.

Lee Beachey walked over to Eldon. "Son, what's weighing on your mind?"

"Well, Dad, I think it's time Ellen came to some decision regarding our relationship. Is she just playing games with me? I told her I thought she might be dating Lamar simply to keep from loneliness. Now I wonder if I did the right thing?"

"Son, I doubt I've ever shared this with you. Before marrying your biological mother, I needed to decide between two young ladies. In time, the Lord led me to your mother who was a precious gem worth the wait. My only regret is that our time together was cut so short by her untimely death when you were four years old.

Making a lifetime decision regarding marriage is not that easy, son. What's it been—a mere five weeks since she left?"

"Yeah, but it seems like forever. We talked so much about our future when she was here that I assumed she would go home and dispense with Lamar within a week or two. That hasn't happened. I'm not sure how much longer I can wait."

His father gave his shoulder a squeeze. "Eldon, it's your life. I believe God will show you what to do if you let him. It's only a suggestion, but I would encourage you to be patient."

Eldon sighed deeply and stood erect. "I guess I did have time to sort out my feelings before ending my relationship with Rosalie. I need to give Ellen the same consideration."

Cleaning out the rest of the barnyard was accomplished with considerable speed.

Coming home from school late Monday afternoon, Ellen checked the dining room table for mail. She wasn't disappointed. Her pulse accelerated as she picked up his familiar script. The letter would dispel the tiredness she felt after another MSU exam.

His letter began with an amusing description of bailing hay. He'd make an excellent farmer if he wasn't preparing for some kind of ministry. She kept reading.

She frowned and her shoulders slumped. Tears spilled down her cheeks as the tiredness of the day washed over her. She whispered under her breath, "No, No." *So, he thinks I'm using Lamar. Am I, Lord? I thought dating Lamar would help me unscramble my scrambled thoughts regarding my future.*

She grabbed a tissue and lay back on her bed. She had a lot of thinking to do.

Ellen's parents exchanged glances throughout dinner. Ellen was quiet and pensive which was unlike her. Yet, they chose not to intrude on her need to sort out whatever was troubling her.

She retreated to her bedroom to study.

Daniel and Francis worked together to clear the dishes.

"Ellen sure was quiet tonight," Daniel said. "What's bothering her?"

"She seemed fine until she received another letter from Eldon. Something's not right."

The Yoders paused to pray. "Lord you know our concern for Ellen," Daniel said. "It seems to be something of grave importance. We lay it out before you, asking for peace of mind for our daughter. In Jesus' name, Amen."

"Amen," echoed Francis.

They completed the evening chores and left for a meeting at church, leaving their daughter in the capable hands of God.

Eldon stopped at the bank on his way home from class on Monday to secure ten dollars' worth of quarters. Dinner held little appeal for him. He had a phone call to make. The only way to assure privacy would be to retrace the ten miles to the village of Shipshewana where he could find a pay phone. He had no desire to have his younger siblings just "happen to hear" this conversation via the house phone.

He watched the clock. At seven-forty-five, he stepped through the living-room archway. "Mom, Dad. I'll be out for a little while. I'm making a run to Ship, but I'll be back in about an hour."

His father looked over the top of the newspaper. "Take care. We'll see you after a while." Eldon was grateful that his father chose not to comment on his unusual trip to town.

Concentration was a fiasco. As the clock struck eight, Ellen tried once more to reread the next day's assignments. She couldn't get the words of the text to stay in focus and closed the book with a bang and rested her head on a stack of other books.

The phone rang. "Hello, Yoders. Ellen speaking."

She could hear coins clinking and a telephone operator said, "You may go ahead and place your call, sir."

A deep bass voice at the other end of the connection said, "Good evening, Sparkie." It was Eldon's pet name for her. Was he calling to end their relationship? Her insides shook.

"Are you okay, Spark?" There was a weighty silence.

She hung on to her stomach. "I think so."

"Ellen, I am calling to discuss the last letter I sent. I was hasty in my judgment of you, and I want to apologize. I was insensitive to your need for time to discern what direction our relationship should take. Will you forgive me?"

She exhaled a quivering breath. "You're forgiven." Her voice was soft and mellow. She ran her fingers through the back of her long hair to dislodge any tangles.

"Saturday, I was working with my dad. He helped me see that such a decision is not easy. He encouraged me to be patient."

She chuckled nervously. "So, your father cautioned you to be patient. Recently, my Mom encouraged me to make a decision soon before I become totally confused. Isn't it interesting how perceptive parents can be?"

The operator came back on the phone line. "Please deposit coins for more minutes or end your call."

Ellen heard more coins drop as he fed the greedy payphone.

"Are you still there?" Eldon asked.

"I'm still here."

She decided to share her heart. "Eldon, I've wanted to make a decision many times over the past few weeks. Then doubts would resurface. I thought the Lord might be allowing those doubts so I wouldn't forget about foreign missions. Yet I'm perfectly comfortable serving him stateside. It would be so much easier if you were here and we could talk face to face."

"Are you asking me to come for a visit soon rather than waiting until the close of summer school?" He sounded hopeful.

"Would you be able to come during semester break? I know my parents would like to meet you."

"Semester break is only a week and a half away. Would that work for your family?"

"I'm sure it would. Can you hold one moment? My parents are coming in the door after a meeting at church."

She put her hand over the receiver while the operator asked for more quarters.

Ellen returned the receiver to her ear. "Eldon, Mom and Pop say they would be happy to host you during the semester break."

"Then I'll be there! How can I find you?"

Ellen gave him detailed directions to her home once he reached the Missula city limits.

They talked freely for a few minutes.

"Before we run out of time and I run out of quarters," Eldon said. "I'd like to reassure you. My love for you hasn't diminished. Rather, it's because of that love and because I thought you'd almost reached a decision that I became impatient. I'm very eager to see you again."

"I've come to care for you a great deal, as well. I'll be counting the days and hours until you come."

"Your time is up," said the impertinent operator.

"Goodnight, dearest."

"Goodnight, Eldon." The phone went dead. She couldn't restrain her smile.

CHAPTER THIRTY-EIGHT

*E*llen dropped her books and sank into a chair. It had been a tedious day at school. Why study for a History of Civ or World Lit exam when Eldon's visit was only ten days away? At the moment, Euripides and Socrates couldn't hold a candle to real life. She needed to get in touch with Lamar. It may not be proper for a girl to call the young man she's dating, but neither is it fair to avoid telling him about Eldon's fast-approaching visit.

Lord, let him be in the office. She dialed and heard someone pick up the phone.

"Pine Lake Camp. Lamar speaking."

Thank ya, Jesus. "Hello, Lamar. I apologize for calling you during working hours."

"There's no need to apologize. It's great to hear from y'all."

She could hear the joy in his voice and cringed.

"Lamar, we agreed to be honest with each other from the beginning." She thought she heard him inhale. "Eldon is coming to meet my parents during semester break which is a little over a week away. It seemed only fair that I let you know."

"Ellen, from the very first evening I met you, I was certain you were the young lady I wanted to marry. For three years I had plenty of time to think about the character traits I needed and hoped for in my future bride. You have all those characteristics." He stopped. Someone had entered the office.

She wondered what else he might have said.

"Ellen, thanks for alerting me about the coming visit. If I had even a few hours off before he comes, I'd want to see you. However, I need to cover the administration since our director is on vacation this week. Would you consider going on a date the evening after Eldon leaves?"

If God was directing her to say goodbye to Lamar, she needed to do it face-to-face and not on the phone.

"Lamar, I'll do that. I think we need to make some decisions. Until then, have a good day."

She hung up the phone with a gentle touch. Ellen pressed her eyelids together, too late to keep tears from seeping past her eyelashes. She hadn't set out to hurt Lamar. She cared for him as a dear friend. But at this moment, she had the distinct feeling that her heart was turning north of the Mason Dixon.

Dearest Ellen,

Each time I think about my last letter, I feel even more ashamed that I misjudged your motives in dating Lamar. Again, I'm sorry for my impatience. I'm also praying for God's leading in our lives.

My thoughts roll on and on. My feelings run deep and deeper with time. Do I doubt? NO! I love you and I am very eager to see you. Soon!

With much love,

Eldon

Dear Eldon,

I have an hour before my next class. I'm sitting on a flat stone slab, sheltered under the canopy of an immense magnolia. It's a "Huck Finn" kind of day with blue skies, a cool breeze, and a brilliant sun. Across campus, the chapel chimes are playing, "Beautiful Dreamer." I'd rather dream than study. I wish you were here.

Your phone call had a tremendous calming effect on my inner turmoil. Your feelings of impatience do not trouble me. If anything, they bring healing where another young man once brought hurt. You've given me the courage to want to learn to love again.

I didn't realize how strongly Lamar felt until I told him about your coming visit. The last thing I wanted to do was to hurt him. Come praying all three of us will understand God's will. I look forward to your visit.

May God keep you safe,
Ellen

CHAPTER THIRTY-NINE

The buzzer rang at five o'clock. The last class of the afternoon was finally over. As far as Eldon was concerned, the professor could have dismissed class five minutes after they convened. He'd mapped out the route to Mississippi the night before, and now he scanned the three by five card in his hand, familiarizing himself with the major routes between Shipshewana and Missula.

Dinner was ready the minute Eldon entered the house. Lee Beachey led the blessing. "Father, we thank you for this food that Mom prepared for us. We pray especially that you would watch over Eldon as he drives many miles throughout the night to see his friend in Mississippi. We trust you will go before him and bless his visit with Ellen and her family. In Jesus' name we pray, Amen." He looked up at Eldon.

"Well son, what time are you planning to leave?"

"How about thirty minutes ago?" Eldon bantered.

His sixteen-year-old brother rolled his eyes. "Wow, Dad. He's got it bad."

"Your time's coming, little brother."

"Not me. No girl is worth driving most of the night plus all day just to meet her family."

"Eldon," his mother said, "what time do you plan to leave? You've been up since five this morning."

"Ellen wrote she would rather have me alive than dead. So, I thought I'd get a few hours of sleep and leave around eleven o'clock. By then there should be less traffic, and I'll be able to make better time."

"Sounds like a plan," Lee said.

After dinner, Eldon tossed some clothes into a weekender and settled in for a minimum of two hours of sleep. He tossed, beating his pillow into a more comfortable wedge. With every turn, he'd catch a glimpse of the clock radio. A gleaming seven-thirty flipped into view. This was worse than useless.

In a matter of minutes, he loaded his skimpy luggage into the trunk of the Corvair.

Lee had been cultivating corn in the field bordering the lawn when he noticed his son preparing to leave. He stopped the tractor and strode toward the car.

"Aren't you leaving a bit early? Will you be safe without any more sleep?"

"I know it's early, but I couldn't sleep. My mind keeps racing, so I might as well be putting some miles behind me."

Lee nodded. "I understand. Please be careful. Stop and rest if you get sleepy."

"I will if I'm not safe to drive." Eldon couldn't imagine getting sleepy. He was a man on a mission.

With a thoughtful gaze, Lee watched the car turn onto the road. *I wonder what this weekend will bring for Eldon? Intense disappointment, or untold joy? Lord, let it be the latter.*

CHAPTER FORTY

For three hours, Eldon battled Friday night traffic until he was south of several major cities. Now, life stretched before him like the open highway. He silenced the distraction of the radio and question after question poured into his mind.

Would this trip end it all or would Ellen and he have a joyful reunion? He'd never met her family and he couldn't help wondering if they'll be compatible or would it be like meeting Rosalie's family who scarcely acknowledged his existence? Would it take a long time to feel comfortable with her family?

What if they didn't approve of him?

Where's Lamar in this whole scenario?

More importantly, what does Ellen think and feel by now? After dating Lamar again, would she be aloof like she was when she returned from meeting him during spring break? Does she plan to keep dating Lamar through the rest of the summer?

Multiple negative, fear-laced thoughts permeated Eldon's thinking for the first half of the trip. But something propelled him to keep driving south throughout the unending night. With police patrolling the highway, he exercised caution to stay within speed limits.

Dawn approached and he began to struggle with highway hypnosis.

I need to stop somewhere to shave and wake up. A gas station appeared on the horizon and he circled to the first available pump.

An enterprising attendant pumped his gas and checked the oil. "Ah, sir, your fan belt is badly twisted. Shall I replace it?" the attendant queried.

Eldon grinned. "Thanks for your concern, but I always carry a spare. If it comes off, I know how to replace it."

It took a scant fifteen minutes to freshen up and eat. He was grateful for his mom's thoughtfulness in sending food. He wouldn't need to waste time or money in looking for a restaurant.

Checking the map, he calculated that he still had a six-hour journey ahead of him. He'd told Ellen he hoped to arrive by two or three p. m. If all goes well, he should be able to get through Tennessee and part of Mississippi to arrive on time.

Awake and alert, he headed back on the road. The air-cooled engine picked up its whirr as he pushed it to seventy miles per hour. His thoughts evolved from despair to hope. Maybe he stood a chance to win her love. Would she be open to going steady?

The Corvair's engine worked to climb the steep hills of Tennessee. The heights served to lift his spirits even higher as he navigated hairpin curves on the four-lane highway. Without warning, brake lights appeared all around him on the crowded highway. Traffic came to a total standstill. Eldon was caught in the center of a horrendous traffic jam.

An hour passed with no movement. Edna's cooler of food was a life-saver.

Thirty minutes later, traffic began to crawl. He had no way of notifying Ellen. Stopping to find a bank to obtain a pocket of quarters to call from a pay phone would only delay him further. He kept driving, sometimes at a snail's pace through small country towns with speed limits of twenty-five-to thirty-miles per hour. This was going to take forever.

He whizzed past the "Welcome to Mississippi" sign which meant he'd be on the road another three hours. Adrenaline surged through him. He was in her home state.

Eldon sat up straight and clamped both hands on the steering wheel. He'd make time.

On long stretches of empty two-lanes, he pushed the engine to eighty. Enthusiasm for what lay ahead deleted any driving inhibitions. Whenever he spotted a slow-moving vehicle in the distance, he decelerated to sixty-five and passed at the first opportunity. Rural Mississippi drivers did not appear to be in a hurry to get anywhere.

Ellen and her mother cleaned the house from stem to stern. They'd finished their food preparations in advance. By mid-afternoon, Francis suggested they sit down to relax.

Ellen sank into the living room wing-backed chair which faced the front picture window. She planned to keep an eye on the entrance of their long gravel driveway while attempting to read. Her mind meandered to the delightful time they would have together. She could hardly wait to introduce him to her parents.

An hour passed. "Mom, Eldon's never late. Do you think something happened to him?"

"I don't think so. He's probably delayed because of summer road construction." Francis sounded optimistic, yet stole surreptitious glances at her watch as she crocheted another round on a delicate doily.

Daniel came in from the barn to shower and joined them. "What time did you say this special young man was coming?"

"Eldon hoped to be here between two and three o'clock. It's four p. m., and he's still not here, which is very unusual for him. I'm afraid he may have been in an accident. I wish he had some means of calling us." Ellen had abandoned all thought of reading over an hour ago. She straightened a stack of magazines and plumped a couch pillow. She chewed her lip.

"Oh, Betsy, he'll be here soon. Traffic can be heavy on a weekend, and you know how Mississippi drivers can slow down progress." Her mother stood. "I'm going to go check on the food."

Ellen didn't leave her post. Cars, trucks and pickups passed in a steady stream out on the highway. No one stopped to turn into the Yoder drive. Her stomach was tied in a hard knot.

Signs to Missula finally appeared. Entering the old southern town with its awesome mansions and massive magnolias catapulted Eldon into the environment Ellen had adopted as home.

Ellen's directions were easy to follow. He was to drive through town. Her last letter indicated he would encounter six bridges after the southern city limits. The Yoder's drive would be immediately after the sixth bridge. What he didn't anticipate was those bridges coming in rapid succession. He had just passed the fifth bridge when the sixth loomed ahead of him. He braked. There was a white mailbox with a distinct sign, "Yoder's Antique Restoration." *This must be the right house since her father is a craftsman.*

He gulped. After pushing all night and most of the day, he was here. *What will I find? Ellen did invite me to meet her parents, but will she be eager to see me?*

Doubt raised its menacing head again as he proceeded with caution.

The grandfather clock struck five.

"Mom, Pop—he's here!"

A white Corvair came to an abrupt stop and turned into the entrance. It was progressing very slowly up the winding drive and halted near the edge of the lawn.

Daniel, Francis, and Ellen sprang into action. They made their way into the breezeway of the white bungalow. Ellen felt shy now that he had arrived. She wanted him to like her parents.

Her father stepped forward. He was a fairly tall man with a slight build. He walked with a decided limp from an old knee injury, his face alight with welcome. Nearing the car, he greeted their guest. "Hello. Hello. You must be Eldon Beachey. Do come in. I am Ellen's father, Daniel Yoder."

Eldon climbed out of the car only to be engulfed in a big bear hug.

Mr. Yoder's hug initiated an immediate bond between Eldon and this gracious, gentle man. They walked to the house together.

Francis was a bit more restrained, giving him a side hug.

Eldon couldn't decipher Ellen's expression. It seemed to be a mix of welcome and concern. What was she thinking? What was she feeling? Her smile looked strained and her forehead was furrowed. He wondered if they would have a future together. Had he driven all this way for nothing? Surely not.

She reached out to take his hand. "Welcome. You must be very tired. Were my directions confusing, making it hard to find us? I was so worried that something might have happened to you." She appeared close to tears.

Oh, she was worried! She does care. Maybe there was a glimmer of hope for them.

"No, your directions were fine. I just got stopped in traffic for an hour and a half. I would have called but it would have delayed me even further."

She sighed and the worry lines in her forehead disappeared. "I understand. I'm so relieved you got here safely."

They walked to the car to retrieve his luggage. "I hope my parent's welcome didn't make you uncomfortable. I know it's different from your family."

"Uncomfortable? No." He grinned. "Just surprised."

Dinner was an event. The Yoder table was laden with southern fried chicken, mounds of mashed potatoes, gravy, vegetables, a salad and fresh baked dinner rolls accompanied with strawberry jam.

After the blessing, Eldon was included in the conversation with references to his grandparents and parents whose lives had intersected with the Yoders in previous generations. In keeping with typical Mississippi Mennonite custom the meal concluded with homemade ice cream and pecan pie. Eldon began to relax a bit in the accepting atmosphere of this family's hospitality.

After dinner, Ellen checked with Eldon, "Should we go for a drive? It's still daylight. We could drive out to see my brother's dairy farm and stop by the hospital for a tour, if you're interested."

"That sounds like a great idea." Eldon found concentration difficult. He wanted and feared, private time with Ellen. If she was going to delay a decision regarding their relationship, he wanted to know it sooner rather than later.

The three-mile drive to her brother's farm was filled with friendly surface talk. Being a former dairy farmer at heart, Eldon could appreciate her brother's farm with an innovative milking parlor. But what he really needed was time to talk.

"Is there a place we could just stop and talk for a while?" He asked.

"Certainly. I know a beautiful, quiet spot. I'm sure the folks at Shalom Baptist wouldn't mind if we use their parking lot."

Dusk had descended on the well-lit church yard. Eldon parked under a light and opened his window. He turned to her. "Ellen, I've been waiting and longing to know how you are feeling about *us.*"

Her voice was quiet. "Eldon, I've missed you so much."

His chest tightened. "Is Lamar still in the picture?" He had to know.

"Yes and no. Yes, in that he asked me to promise I would see him one more time, no matter what the outcome would be of this weekend. And no, he will no longer be involved. I have made the decision to end that relationship." She laid her hand on his arm and looked up at him searching for clues to their future but finding none. Her heart yearned to belong exclusively to Eldon but would he take the slower cautious route of going steady?

His heart hammered inside his chest. He hadn't come with the intent to propose. He was the logical type of male who thought first then took action. Now he knew what he wanted more than anything else in the world.

"Ellen, will you marry me?"

Her face was radiant. "Yes, I would feel honored to become Mrs. Eldon Beachey."

Eldon drew her close. They had waited six long months for this sacred moment. Sealing their engagement with their first kiss left both of them breathless.

Eldon relaxed, murmuring into her hair, "This is too good to be true."

She looked up at him, "But it's true. God has shown us the way."

EPILOGUE

Four Days Later...

Dearest Eldon,

It's nearing midnight, yet sleep eludes me. I came in an hour ago from saying goodbye to Lamar. At last I am free to love you without any reservation. What joy! It's hard to fathom that our wedding day is a mere six months away.

It's difficult for Lamar to accept that God is asking him to give up the girl he thought God had reserved for him. He

*assured me he will respect my decision
and thanked me for telling him now
rather than at the end of the summer.
Please pray with me that God will direct
Lamar's life just as he has ours.
All my love is yours,
Ellen*

Two Years Later...

While attending Moody Bible Institute, Lamar met and married the young woman God had prepared for him. Together, they entered foreign missions while the Beacheys served stateside. God's ways refined each of their lives with a touch of gold.

Thirty-Three Years Later...

Ellen returned to Missula to give her dying father nursing care. The competent black physician caring for Daniel was a specialist in his field and treated her elderly father with utmost dignity.

Forty-Eight Years Later...

While touring the hospital, Ellen and her husband were encouraged seeing white, black, and Choctaw professionals work as a team to deliver quality health care.

THE END

About the Author

Idella Otto holds a B.S. in Nursing and an M.A. in Christian Counseling. She joined her extended family in ministry to Choctaw Indians in Mississippi in the 1960's. Idella and her husband, Emory are presenters for Mennonite & Brethren Marriage Encounter, a national and international ministry. They live in Pennsylvania.

Idella can be reached at idellaotto43@aol.com.